WHISPERS
IN THE
SHADOWS

A Dark Night Thriller
Book 1

JASON LaVELLE

WHISPERS IN THE SHADOWS
A Dark Night Thriller – Book 1
*Copyright © 2018 by Jason LaVelle
Cover Art Copyright © 2018 by D. Robert Pease
*Original Copyright © 2014 under the Title: DELIA

FIRST EDITION SOFTCOVER
ISBN: 1622534549
ISBN-13: 978-1-62253-454-8

Editor: Jessica West
Interior Designer: Lane Diamond

www.EvolvedPub.com
Evolved Publishing LLC
Butler, Wisconsin, USA

Printed in Book Antiqua font.

BOOKS BY JASON LaVELLE

A DARK NIGHT THRILLER
Book 1: *Whispers in the Shadows*
Book 2: *The Cold Room*
Book 3: *The Dark of Night*

DYING WORLD CHRONICLES
Book 1: *Pathosis*
Book 2: *Ecocide*

DEDICATION

For my family,
you are my whole world.

Chapter 1

A gunshot woke Delia from sleep. Her eyes flew open as the loud crack roared through the house, and she bolted upright in bed. She wore a long linen nightshirt, but gooseflesh raced across her body.

The shot came from within the house. She knew because, on occasion, her father had to put down one of the animals outside, which produced a muffled sound. This one sounded like it came from downstairs; the very walls had vibrated with its force.

She jumped out of bed.

Heavy footfalls stomped up the stairs, adding a thumping bassline to the echoes from the gunshot still ringing through the house. A confusing noise filled her head, the type of sound a windstorm made against her bedroom window.

Moments later, a scream bellowed up the stairs and found its way to her room.

She recognized the voice immediately, though something about it sounded terribly wrong.

Her father never screamed like that. His voice was usually soft and kind. A mere word from him offered hope and compassion. Not tonight, though. Tonight, he sounded strained and angry.

"Delia! Delia, come here!"

She hesitated for only a moment, then her feet moved toward the bedroom door.

What's wrong with him?

Her hands shook, but she reached for the door handle anyway. As she pulled the door open, her father burst into the room.

His haggard face frightened her, his eyes wide against his leathery skin. He wore filthy jeans and a white t-shirt stained with dark red splotches.

Is that blood?

Delia's breath hitched in fear.

"Go sit on the bed!" Anger and something else tinged her father's normally kind voice.

Delia obeyed, though she moved slowly, unsure of every step. "Where did that gunshot come from, Daddy?"

"You sit there quietly." Her father fumbled with the shotgun. He pulled a shell from one bulging pocket and attempted to load it into the weapon.

"Where's Momma?"

"Sit quiet, ya hear me?" His clipped words came out loud as he concentrated on the gun.

Something cold and dark settled in the pit of Delia's stomach. She trembled as she repeated, "Where's Mother?"

The shell her father was fumbling with finally slid into place with a loud click, and he sighed with relief.

"She's with our heavenly Father now, Delia." He smiled sadly and cocked the shotgun. "But don't worry, we're going to see her soon." Then he advanced on her.

She felt lightheaded with panic but, strangely, her senses sharpened.

The father she adored took a step toward her and raised the shotgun with trembling arms. The smell of gunpowder mixed with the dirty tang of steel in the air.

Making a split-second decision, she leapt off the bed and dove directly for him, but she wasn't trying to reach for his gun—she wanted to escape. With a spectacular, waterless swan dive, she threw herself into the empty space between his legs, trying desperately to get to the blocked doorway.

She made it halfway through before he slammed them shut against her. His legs clamped down against her hips. "Delia, you mind me now! This is for your own good!"

She ignored him, using all her strength to pull her slender body out from under his grip. Though he tried to pin her in, she wriggled free and shot down the hallway to the stairs.

"Delia!" he screamed madly behind her. He came after her with an uneven lope, but because he was so much bigger, for every two steps she took, he only had to take one.

She made it down the steps without stumbling and somehow made it to the front door. As she reached for the handle, another shot filled the air. She dropped to the ground just as a shot blasted the top of the wooden door into splinters. She pinned herself to the floor for a moment, long enough to see the body of her mother lying motionless on the living room floor.

"Momma," she whimpered.

Fear and heartache clawed their way into her chest and her breaths came fast and hard. Her father had lost his mind. He intended to murder her, and his steps followed closely on the staircase.

Loading the gun had taken him a while last time, and he now plodded down the staircase as if lost.

She had a chance—a slim one—but if she ran, she just might make it to safety.

Delia jumped up and grabbed the door handle. With one last look at her mother's body, she swung open the door and bolted out into the night.

She ran through the backyard toward the field. A glance over her shoulder revealed her father exiting the house. She had to make it to the field before he caught up to her. She could hide in the tall wheat. The great moving sea of pale yellow loomed in the darkness ahead. She kept running, not pausing for a moment when the long stalks of wheat brushed against her arms and face.

Her farm girl's feet were tough and calloused, so the rough clay underfoot didn't hurt. She stopped once, thinking she would hide, but her father came crashing through the wheat in her direction, so she ran as fast as she could—the way she did at school when she was trying to win a race, which she always did. Tag had always been her favorite game, but now she played for her life. She didn't know if she could outrun her father, whose breathing was getting louder behind her, but she had to try.

Her life depended on it.

She ran to the only place she knew, to her only hope. Her aunt and uncle lived on the other side of the field, in a small house with a large yellow barn. Uncle Don lived on the short side of the 200-acre wheat field. Even in the dead of night, his barn loomed ahead in her mind, a safe haven of bright yellow, a beacon of hope—as long as she didn't tire out before making it through the mile of dark field in front of her.

"Delia!" her father called in a panting voice, already tiring.

So was she. Delia's lungs burned with effort, but after being in the field for five minutes, she finally spotted the big sodium light on the top gambrel of Uncle Don's barn.

"Delia, stop right now!"

She wanted to stop. Her lungs were on fire now and her feet felt sticky. She didn't know if the stickiness was from the soft earth or if they were bleeding. The broken stalks of wheat that lay on the ground were razor sharp, and must have been cutting her feet, but her mind focused only on getting to her uncle's house before getting shot.

What if he kills Uncle Don, too?

She couldn't worry about her uncle right now; she just had to get there before her father killed her. A moment later, another shotgun blast rang out, and hot buckshot grazed her arm. Blood immediately flowed from the wound, and she almost stumbled in horror and shock.

He shot me! My own daddy shot me! He shot me!

She pushed on. A wave of nausea churned in her stomach and she vomited in her mouth. With no choice but to continue, she spat out what she could and swallowed the rest, batting away the tears streaming down her cheeks. She had almost made it through the mile of dense wheat field. The light on the barn grew brighter.

Behind her, Daddy cocked the shotgun again.

Then, in mid-stride, Delia burst out of the wheat field and broke into a dead run with all of the strength she had left.

Her father fell out of the field a moment later. "Stop running right now, Delia! You're going to see your mother! We'll all be together!"

Delia was only a dozen yards from the back porch of the house when she hit the knee-high manure-spreading cart. In the black of night, the dark red hunk of metal had been invisible. She ran straight into it, cartwheeled over the top, and landed on her shoulder. Her vision blurred momentarily, and she gasped to suck in a breath, only to start screaming as her father reached her.

"You," he huffed, "need," another deep breath, "to mind your father."

Delia couldn't hold back the tears. They poured from her eyes as she sobbed uncontrollably. "Why, Daddy? Why do you want to kill me?"

"Not kill you, darling," he said in a soft tone. "I'm saving you." He raised the shotgun and pointed it at her face. "Close your eyes, honey. We'll be with your mother soon."

"John!" A booming voice rang out over the yard.

Delia looked past her father and saw Uncle Don, carrying a long rifle, hurrying toward them. At almost sixty years old, Don was much older than his brother. A massive man, he stood six-foot-five and easily weighed three hundred pounds. Everyone liked and respected Uncle Don.

"Go back inside, Donald. This is no business of yours! This is my family business."

"John! Goddammit, brother, don't make me put a bullet in you. You get away from that little girl right now."

"You don't understand, Don."

"I do. We've all had hard times. We've all hit rock bottom at some time or another. All we can do is keep on trucking, keep fighting the good fight."

"Missy is dead."

"Jesus," Don whispered. "Let your daughter go, John. We can take care of her."

"No one's taking care of her but me. I told you, Don, this is family business."

Delia's dad turned back to her and cocked the shotgun's hammer.

A bullet blew out the front of his chest, showering Delia with a heavy spray of blood as her daddy fell to the ground.

Uncle Don walked over and stood above him. "She *is* my family."

Chapter 2

One wouldn't appreciate a funeral on a nice day, but the dark gray skies and drizzle of rain that fell on the small group made the occasion especially dismal. John and Missy Jensen—not well-known but not reclusive, either—had gone to church every Sunday and always exchanged friendly handshakes with their fellow parishioners. Only twenty or so mourners showed up at the internment. Delia stood a few feet in front of her aunt. She stared ahead at the twin coffins sitting next to two holes in the ground.

Behind her, Aunt Deb spoke to a friend of the family—not loudly, but Delia heard every word nonetheless. Not that any of the gossip surprised her. Her aunt and uncle had been as forthcoming as they could be.

"So, you decided to keep the girl then?"

"We did. Donald just couldn't put her out after all she's been through."

"Where will she sleep?"

"We bunked her in with Lilly. They get along all right, considering."

"Has she said much about what happened that night?"

"She hasn't spoken at all."

"About her father or not at all?"

"She hasn't spoken at all, Judy, not a single word.

She doesn't cry. She doesn't complain. She doesn't speak at all. It's like the whole thing has made her go mute."

"My goodness."

"Indeed. The child went through something horrible and I'm not sure that she's going to be okay."

"You think the crazy might run in her blood?"

"I hope not. We'll watch her carefully. The bank was taking the farm from John. He'd been struggling for years and, apparently, the loan man finally had enough. Said they were going to take the land, the farm, the house, the animals, everything. He wouldn't even be able to keep his truck when they were done with him."

"It's really no wonder he went off his rocker, I suppose."

Aunt Deb shook her head. "It's a very sad business. Those bankers don't care who they're hurting."

"Why didn't he come to you for help? Surely, Donald could have helped in some way. That's not to say it was your responsibility, of course."

"Just before Don shot him, John told him no one was going to be taking care of his family but him. We're supposin' he thought that if he couldn't take care of his family, they were better off dead."

"My Lord, he truly was crazy, wasn't he?"

"Uh-huh."

The First Presbyterian Church sat quietly in the distance. From the small house next to it, the pastor emerged and walked toward the cemetery where they waited.

"Women," a deep voice growled under his breath. "Quiet yourselves, now. Be respectful of the dead in this place."

"I'm sorry, Don."

"Don't go spreading this business around further. The girl is going to have a rough enough go of it."

Uncle Donald had saved her. He worked hard and made a good living as a veterinarian and farrier. They'd paid off the mortgage on their house years ago.

The pastor made it over to the fresh gravesite and greeted them all. He took the time to softly shake Delia's hand and offered her a well-practiced condoling smile. Then he spoke about life and death. He talked a little about God's fury, then about redemption. He spoke about forgiveness for a long time. He reminded them that God alone should be the judge of any man.

"Remember, my good people, that we have lost two of our flock today, but that there is still one of that family remaining, one that will need all of the kindness and support we can offer."

Self-conscious, Delia flushed as all the eyes of the congregation turned to her.

"Remember that a child especially needs warmth in times of cold, and mercy in times of heartache." The pastor gave Delia another small smile.

A prick of emotion welled up in her chest. She tried to choke it down, but it kept coming up, threatening to overflow from her eyes. She pressed her hands against the side of her face and tried to concentrate on anything else but this.

As the priest continued to speak, two men lowered her mother's casket into the cold black hole.

Delia hiccupped silent little sobs. She tried to muffle the sound because she didn't want them to think her weak. She wanted them to see her as strong. Nevertheless, the tears came and she could do nothing to restrain them. Hurt and abandoned by the parents she loved, Delia's heart overflowed with grief. Her breathing became ragged and she took great heaving gasps. Even then, she couldn't get enough air in her lungs.

An arm settled around her, and the rich smell of leather soothed her. She looked up and Uncle Don peered down at her, with his meaty arm holding her next to him. Even for a tall girl she barely came up past his large stomach

He turned Delia in to face him, and held her close to his body.

Delia buried her face against him.

He spoke softly. "There, no one can see your tears now."

The tears poured. After a few moments, a large circle of Delia's tears grew on Don's plaid button-down shirt.

Embarrassed, Delia couldn't stop the flow, her chest heaving and hitching with effort.

As the grave men pulled up the ropes from her mother's lowered casket, he held her. Soon, her father would make his way down into the ground as well.

Delia eventually regained control of her breathing, and the tears stopped coming. She wiped the back of her hand over her face and turned away from Don.

Her father's casket began its descent.

She felt great anger towards him, but more than that—confusion. Why would everything have been so bad without the farm, anyway? Her mother had always said, "Home is where the heart is." They could have gone anywhere as long as they were together. But her father had to go and ruin it.

Images from that night overwhelmed her: her mother on the living room floor; her gray, lifeless face; and the puddle of blood surrounding her.

The emotions rose again. More tears formed.

Then a warm hand took hers. The new hand was soft and little.

Uncle Don still stood on one side of her with his arm around her back.

Her cousin Lilly, Uncle Don and Aunt Deb's daughter, stood at her side.

They'd be more like sisters now. Lilly—only five years old—quietly looked up at Delia with sparkling blue eyes and smiled.

Delia returned the smile. She stood like that, just looking at Lilly's small, perfect face, while they finished lowering her father into the ground. She would not go look over the edge of the grave. She would not throw a shovelful of dirt. Instead, as the pastor closed his Bible and dismissed the mourners, Delia walked hand in hand with Lilly back to the truck. They did not speak, but a connection formed between Delia and the small girl.

They sat together in the bed of the old pickup as Don drove them home. When they returned to the house, Aunt Deb pulled her aside. "There are going to be some people coming over, all right? We'll have lunch, and then you can be dismissed if you'd like."

Delia nodded her understanding.

"They're all going to want to talk to you, ya know. It would be nice if you could speak to them."

Delia said nothing in response. She went up to her shared bedroom to put on a more comfortable dress. She had squeezed into the same black one from her grandmother's wake and funeral last year, but her body just wasn't the same now.

She pulled a simple cloth dress over her pale flesh and sat in the room to wait until her aunt called her downstairs. The room seemed small for two girls, but she felt safer than she would have alone. Every night since her parents' death she'd woken up with nightmares.

She brushed her fingernails back and forth against the smooth wood of the bedroom floor.

Steps on the porch outside and voices from beyond the window echoed up to her.

She looked out the bedroom window and saw a small procession of people approaching.

She sighed deeply and cinched the cloth belt around her waist. Then she made her way through the house to where people she had met at one time or another but barely knew waited to see her.

They all wanted to look at the girl whose father tried to kill her. Whispers followed Delia through the house. She tried several times to stand still, but their eyes kept turning toward her, some with pity, some with disdain, and so she shuffled silently from room to room.

Unable to hide or to stand another minute of the quiet assault, she wandered out into the yard where Lilly swung herself on the swing set.

Delia sat next to Lilly on a swing.

Lilly held out her hand again for Delia.

Delia smiled at her and took the offered hand.

Then Lilly spoke to her. "You're going to be my best friend now, Delia." Then she released Delia's hand and went back to pushing her little feet to move the swing.

Everything changed after that. Delia was the same, but different. She didn't feel things the way she used to. Playing with other children was no longer fun. Sad things didn't bring her sorrow. Her father had flipped a switch within Delia and somehow turned part of her off, like when one of her body parts fell asleep. She could still feel, but in a muffled way.

***

The weekend of mourning ended and Delia returned to school, but not for long. Three school days passed with her sitting silently, refusing to speak to her teachers, before they deemed her "excused" for the year. They only had two weeks left anyway. The school principal did have some opinions on Delia that he shared with Aunt Deb.

"Sure, she's been through hell," he said, "but the girl needs to be disciplined. Give her a good tanning and she'll snap right out of this."

Delia sat in the corner of the room while this conversation took place. She heard everything, of course, but then she thought she heard something else.

A far-off whisper grew closer to her.

As the principal spoke—his fat red face working out his judgments against her—the whispers became louder in Delia's ears until it felt like she had a conch shell pressed to her head, listening to the sound of the ocean. Delia looked around the room for the source of the sound, but none presented itself. The sound made concentrating on the principal's words difficult, but his snide remarks came through nonetheless.

He told Aunt Deb that she needed to figure out something before the next school year or Delia couldn't return.

Aunt Deb nodded and said, "That's fine."

As Deb led her out of the building, the quiet of the countryside replaced the whispering. Deb drove her back to the house in Don's truck. She didn't scold Delia, nor did she look angry with her. Her aunt remained silent until they pulled back into the driveway. She shifted the truck out of gear but let the engine idle.

"I saw someone die once," Aunt Deb said.

Delia looked up at her in surprise.

"It was a boy I knew when I was little, my first boyfriend, I guess. We played in the woods often, just doing as kids will do. One day we went climbing trees. He climbed much farther than I could, much higher than I ever would." She paused to glance at Delia. "A branch broke when he was climbing down. He fell straight through to the ground and landed on his noggin. I remember how his head bent sideways. I remember the sound it made. His neck went purple. Even as a youngin' I knew he was dead."

She looked over at Delia and shut off the engine.

"It was awful. I had nightmares for days. I know you'll heal from this, and I know it'll be difficult. We'll do everything we can to help you."

Delia nodded to her.

"Keep up on your chores and help with the cooking and things will be fine, okay?" Deb patted her on the leg.

Delia wandered out away from the house while Lilly napped. She knew the area well, since she grew up just on the other side of the field, but she could still explore further and find new places. She walked up to the edge of the wheat field, letting her outstretched hands brush along the warm stalks as she did. She impulsively ducked into the rows of wheat and disappeared.

Once in the field, she moved more quickly, walking in the direction of her old house. Delia brushed wheat from her face as she trod, then began to run. She ran then ran faster. She remembered that night, running from her father. Now she ran from the emptiness she felt inside. She ran as hard as she could, until her lungs were bursting and tears rolled down her face.

"Father!" she screamed out into the wind. "Father!"

No sooner had she screamed, she tumbled out of the field and into her old yard. She fell onto her knees and let herself cry. The tears came streaming down her face and her breathing hitched in her chest, then giant sobs barked out of her throat. She couldn't stop crying or move away so she lay down on the grass. Her bawling turned to soft sobs that soon stopped altogether. Her weary mind demanded rest, and Delia fell asleep on the lawn.

Her father came to her in a dream.

Delia opened her eyes. The rich smell of grass and the earth beneath it filled her nostrils. She raised her head and saw him walking toward her from the house.

"Dee," he said, smiling, using his own special name for her.

"Father!" she cried, and rose from the grass to meet him.

He walked toward her as she got up.

Delia ran up as if to throw her arms around him, but stopped.

"Is mother here too?"

"No, dear. Mother is in heaven where she belongs."

Delia's face dropped.

"What about you? Where are you?"

Her father smiled sadly. "I'm nowhere. I'm caught in the in-between. I'll be here for some time."

"Why, father? Why did you do this to me?" Her face grew warm with an angry flush, tears not far behind. "I'm all alone now!"

John's ghostly head bowed down in shame. "I'm sorry, Dee. I lost all sense of what I was supposed to be."

"What do you mean?"

"I was supposed to be a good husband and a good father, no matter what. I failed. I was weak, Delia. You can never be weak in this life, or it will destroy you."

"It was those bankers' fault, wasn't it, father?" Tears dripped from her face.

Her father wrapped his arms around her in a tight embrace.

His warm body and the rough skin of his hands on the back of her neck consoled Delia as nothing else could.

After a moment, her father held her at arm's length and stroked the side of her face. "It was my fault, Delia. You can never be like me. I did all the wrong things. I didn't use my head. I followed dreams instead of my brain." He cupped her face in his hands. "I didn't do what was necessary to take care of my family and I lost everything. Now, I've taken everything from you."

"I don't know if I understand, father."

"You can't always follow your dreams. Sometimes you have to listen to your head more than your heart. Delia, you have to be the best at everything you do. It's the only way to make it in the world."

Delia nodded meekly at his words.

Her father released her face and took a step back from her. "I love you, Dee. You have to get out of here. Get away from the farm. Those city folks have it good. Don't blame the bankers for what happened to us. I should have tried to be more like them all along."

She was so confused. This didn't sound like what mother had always told her.

"Will you ever come back here?"

"I think I must," replied her father.

"Then I'll be able to visit you sometimes?"

"I don't know that. I have to go for now."

"But I don't want you to go, father.

"I'm sorry, Dee, it's time for you to wake up now."

She reached out to him and held his calloused hand in hers.

He smiled softly at her, but his pale blue eyes seemed sad and far away.

Chapter 3

The sound of loud machinery woke her.

Delia peeled her face off the lawn. The grass she slept on grew slightly damp and stuck to her cheek. She looked up toward the sound.

A large tractor pulled a harvest combine up to the side of the field.

Who would be trying to harvest her field, her family's wheat?

She gestured angrily at the man driving the tractor. She waved her arms back and forth, but he could not see her. Finally, she ran up to him. When she got right up alongside the tractor, he noticed her and startled.

He slowed the tractor's progress and Delia pointed to the field and shook her head vehemently.

The man looked over his shoulder and pointed behind him. With that, he geared up the tractor once more and started the harvester.

Delia looked behind her to where the man had pointed.

A black sedan sat parked on the lawn. A short round man dressed for church in a big city stepped out.

"What are you doing here, miss?" he said abruptly, walking toward her.

Delia just glared at him and pointed toward the house.

Realization dawned on the man's face.

"Oh, yes, you're the little girl who lived here. I see." The man sighed. "This isn't your house, anymore. This is the bank's house now. I'm sorry, dear."

He did not look sorry to Delia. In fact, he actually looked happy.

She pointed out to the field.

"Your father owed us a great deal of money. We're taking the house and the harvest as payment for his debt. Don't bother that man again. He's only doing his job."

The nicely-dressed man stepped within a few feet of Delia and her head filled with a strange swishing sound like someone whispering in her ear.

Delia looked for the source, but saw only the man on the tractor.

The bank man grew closer—within reaching distance—and the whispering—no real words, just air rushing around in her head—increased in volume.

The man looked Delia up and down. He stood too close.

She could smell his thick cologne. His red face was punctuated by deep pockmarks, and the familiar scent of alcohol wafted over to her. She didn't like this man.

"I'll tell you what, dear, you get in the car with me, and I'll bring you back to where you belong." The man smiled brightly and reached out for her arm.

Delia jerked away from him.

"Come on now, come here," he said sweetly. "I just want to give you a ride. I know this must be tough for you."

The sound in her head rose to a loud buzz, and the man lunged for her. He clamped a meaty red hand over her arm and pulled against her.

Delia immediately bit him, sinking her teeth as far as she could into his hand.

He screamed and released her arm, then grabbed for her hair.

But Delia was running again, and by the time the fat man had his wits about him, she'd already reached the wheat field. She ran until the buzzing in her head quieted to a soft whisper, then to nothing at all. She didn't know which direction she had run, but a tree thirty or forty yards off to her left might help. She would climb it and get her bearings. As she reached the base of the gnarled old cherry, a small voice called out to her.

"Where did you come from?"

Delia jumped and looked up into the tree.

A black-haired boy with no shirt and a dark tan smiled from a craggy branch a few feet above her.

"I'm Francis. What's your name?"

Delia slumped down to the ground and leaned her back against the tree. She took deep, heavy breaths and tried to compose herself. Her heart—already beating madly from running—ached from the boy startling her. She didn't want him to see that she'd been frightened, though. After a few breaths, she calmed herself.

The boy—thin and muscular, like Delia—swung down from the tree and stood in front of her. A long white scar ran from beneath his waistband and up toward his ribs.

"Sorry I startled you." He offered up a smile. The boy looked about her age or a little younger. "I saw you running in the field. Where did you come from?" He curiously looked at her for a moment when she did not answer. "Did you come from the house over there?"

Delia raised her eyebrows a moment then looked down at her dirty knees.

"It looked like someone was chasing you."

Delia nodded.

"Do you want to climb my tree? It's safe up there."

Delia thought of Aunt Deb's story about her friend dying while climbing a tree. Then she stood and started to climb. She had only gotten up six or seven feet when she realized the boy remained on the ground.

He stared up at her and she did not know why for a moment. Then she realized he could see up her skirt.

She had not worn breeches today, so only a slip of underwear covered up her feminine parts. She broke a heavy chunk of bark off the tree and threw it down at him.

He was so distracted by the forbidden fruits between her legs that he didn't notice until the heavy bark smacked into his nose.

"Aw, come on! You didn't have to do that!" He snorted and rubbed his nose.

This elicited an involuntary smile from Delia.

"Sorry," he begrudgingly mumbled.

She climbed a little higher, not caring if he looked, then wedged herself into the crook of two branches.

The boy climbed up next to her. He shimmied a little farther out onto the branch and they sat silently together in the protection of the large tree.

From this vantage point, Delia could see the combine out in the field. She watched as it cut a steady, twenty-foot path out of the wheat.

Down the length of the field it went, almost out of sight, before it hit the end and turned around to start the long journey back. The harvest would take two days.

As she watched the combine tear down what her father had sown—an ocean of golden stalks—a tear welled up in one eye and rolled over her cheek. She quickly batted it away.

The boy had seen.

She hoped he wouldn't say anything and, for a while, he didn't. After watching the combine for nearly an hour, Delia's butt and thighs complained. She prepared to make her way down when the boy spoke.

"That was your house, wasn't it?" He looked toward the home where she had grown up.

Delia looked him in the eyes and nodded slowly.

"We heard about what happened." The boy turned his eyes away from her, back toward the field. "I suppose after that you just don't have anything to talk about at all, huh? Well, I have chores I have to do. I come out this way before dinner a lot. You can share my tree with me again if you want."

Delia nodded to him again.

She glanced over the sea of wheat once more, then clambered down out of the tree. She had a long walk back to the house ahead of her.

She set off through the field, mindful of the direction in which the combine was moving. Getting caught in its path meant certain death.

***

Delia reached the house just in time to help Aunt Deb get dinner on the table.

Aunt Deb gave her a questioning look when she came into the kitchen out of breath and flushed from running, but Delia shrugged it off and set the table right away.

As they sat down to eat, Uncle Don spoke to Delia.

"I want you girls to be careful out in that field. The combine is running and those men are working long hours. Sometimes they don't see everything. It would be a shame if there were an accident out there."

Delia nodded and Lilly said, "Yes, father."

Don glanced over at Deb, who gave him a look full of meaning. "Your aunt received a call from a man who works for the bank. He said you were snooping around the house and that you attacked him when he told you they had to take the house away."

Delia shook her head vehemently, but her uncle held up his hand and continued. "Delia, I know that was your house. I'm not angry. Just stay out of there, okay? The bank man said he would call the police if he caught you over there again."

Delia nodded her compliance but she was fuming within. That man from the bank had grabbed her. She'd known he meant to do her harm.

That was why she bit him.

Chapter 4

The next day found Delia back in the tree. She beat Francis there so she could see which direction he came from. As she scanned the horizon, he eventually appeared, walking along a distant tree line. She knew only one house laid in that direction several miles away: the butcher's house. Her father once brought her with him when he'd had a cow processed. Her mother always butchered the chickens herself, but insisted that her father use the butcher for their beef. Mother always said that if not done right, the beef wouldn't keep as long.

Delia didn't remember much about the butcher's house, and she had never met anyone who lived there besides the old man who processed their meat.

Francis looked up into the tree as he approached and smiled at her. He seemed happy to see her there.

"You don't go to school?" he asked.

She shook her head.

"Do you think you'll ever talk again?"

She nodded. No one could stay mute forever, but her thoughts remained too chaotic to form words.

He carefully pulled a paper-wrapped parcel out of a sack he had slung over his shoulder and motioned for her to come down.

She easily hopped out of the tree and stood next to him, clearly at least an inch taller.

"I got a special treat for us," he said, excited and full of mischief. He unwrapped the package and revealed a large piece of golden cornbread.

Her eyes lit up and she smiled broadly. The bread looked moist and delicious.

He broke the piece of cornbread in half and held one piece out to her. When she went to take it, he jerked his hand back playfully.

"For a kiss," he said.

She stared at him.

She thought about hitting him in the stomach and running away before he could catch her. But the cornbread looked so good. She'd not had any cornbread since her mother passed.

***

Her aunt and uncle had indoor plumbing and electricity, but they only bathed twice a week to cut down on cost and wear on their well. The girls would bathe first, one after another, using the same water. Then her aunt would drain and refill the tub so she and uncle Don could bathe.

After dinner, Lilly got into the tub first to scrub the last few days' dust and grime from her little body. Delia waited in the hallway outside the bathroom just as her aunt had instructed her.

"I'm getting out now," Lilly called from the bathroom.

Delia opened the door and let herself in to take her turn.

Lilly stood up in the bathtub, looking at her curiously. Then she stepped over the tall edge of the tub and grabbed one of the rough brown towels her mother had laid out.

Delia pulled off her plain orange dress and dingy grey underwear—filthy from sitting on tree branches with Francis—and tossed them onto the floor. Once she'd stripped naked, she stepped over to the tub.

Lilly still watched her with a strange expression.

Delia paused and looked at her for an answer.

"We usually don't change in front of people," Lilly said softly.

Delia felt Lilly's eyes on her body. Still a child, and not a young woman like Delia had become, Lilly probably noticed the differences between them. A little ashamed of not knowing the rules of bath time, Delia quickly popped into the large, cast iron tub and sank down until the water covered her budding breasts. She was only thirteen, but her body was changing, and she'd only just begun to get used to it herself.

"It's okay. I'm going to be a big girl like you someday. I don't mind that you came in the bathroom. It's just not what we usually do." Lilly gave her a quick but genuine smile then hurried out of the bathroom.

She sighed and closed her eyes. The warm water felt heavenly, and she thought it washed away more than dirt. The clean felt much deeper. A large block of stinky white soap hid at the bottom of the tub where Lilly had left it. She fished it out and scrubbed all over her body. It smelled terrible, a bitter, piney smell that bit at her throat, but she loved the clean feeling as it glided over her skin.

Normalcy seeped into Delia once again. She still felt lost, but not without hope. Funny how a little thing like a bath could make such a difference. She smiled at the ceiling and started to drift off to sleep when her aunt knocked on the door.

"Time to get out, Delia."

***

Nervous energy coursed through him, but Francis remained still. He had spent two hours lying prone on the warm ground, nestled in thick foliage. As the sun set, he began to hear the scurrying of small creatures in the woods. With his tongue, Francis moved the small lump of chewing tobacco he had stolen from his brother beneath his lip. He silently spit out a tarlike stream of tobacco-laced saliva onto the ground next to him. His gums and lips had gone numb where he'd stuffed the coarse mass of chew. The tiny rush of nicotine helped keep him awake and alert.

Finally, he heard the rhythmic thumps he'd been waiting for. He blinked hard to freshen his vision, then lowered his cheek down close to the rifle's stock. Moments later, a fluffy ball of gray appeared upwind of him. He observed the rabbit calmly, laying a short distance from the rabbit's run, so he had only to wait and the rabbit would cross near enough for a guaranteed kill.

He patiently waited for the small creature to make its way toward its den, in a thicket not far from where he lay.

A dozen feet from him, the rabbit stopped and raised its tiny twitching nose in the air. Though he'd remained silent, the rabbit looked right at him. He imagined the creature's beady eyes widened as it saw the .22 pointed its way.

He squeezed the trigger.

***

Francis paused before entering the house. He heard the radio in the sitting room, a large, wooden machine that sat atop an antique table. A gravelly voice purred out through the main floor of the house: the evening bible story hour, something his father never missed. He knew better than to disturb him at this time, not that he would have anyway. Since Francis's mother died, the man known only as the Butcher had withdrawn from his family.

His father's eyes followed Francis as he made his way through the foyer and over to the staircase, then he took to the wooden stairs in darkness. One hand absentmindedly trailed against the wallpaper—roses and lilies—that his mother had hung so long ago. In his other hand, a canvas sack sagged with the weight of the dead rabbit.

In his room, the familiar musky odor greeted him His room didn't consist of much; a twin-size bed against one wall, a window, and a wooden stool with a flat-topped desk on the opposite wall from the bed. At the foot of his bed sat a tall metal foot locker, the type utilized in army barracks, where he kept his clothing. For decoration, he had hung objects of varying importance to him on the plaster-lath walls.

He flung the sack onto his desk, where it landed with a muted thud.

His eyes burned with tiredness, but he stayed up anyway. He had work to do, and it couldn't wait. He lit the kerosene lamp on his desk and a warm orange glow filled his room. Their house had electricity, but not upstairs. Only the kitchen and sitting room had been wired for invisible power.

He opened the metal footlocker that served as his dresser and foraged through the clothing until he found his favorite tool—a long, gnarled hunting knife — ugly, but with an edge as fine as a razor. Francis tested the sharpness by lightly tapping the blade against the end of his thumbnail, satisfied when it stuck slightly.

He sat astride his wooden stool and began to work, humming a song his mother used to sing to him and his brother on occasion. His hands moved deftly over the table and the long blade glinted in the light. The rabbit came apart before him and as it did, he started singing, his small, tenor voice both melodious and haunting in the warmly-lit room.

> *"Shades of night are creeping*
> *Willow trees are weeping*
> *Old folks and babies are sleeping*
> *Silver stars are gleaming*
> *All alone I'm scheming*
> *Scheming to get you out here*
> *My dear"*

He also thought of the girl he met, Delia.

He smiled as he sang. He didn't have friends, it had been a blessing that he had met her-- a gift from God, his mother would have said. He had gotten a kiss today, and he liked it. He already wanted to see her again. In fact, he *needed* to see her.

Francis paused his work and sighed, exhausted. The blood-slicked knife slipped out of his hand and clattered loudly onto the desk. He froze.

His brother never slept this early, and even the slightest provocation would bring him out of his room and into Francis's.

After the last time, Francis had been sore for a week. He didn't want to repeat that any time soon, or ever.

After two minutes of breathing heavily and remaining as motionless as possible, Francis picked the knife back up. He made several more cuts, then gently set the knife down.

Finished. Good. He was so tired.

Francis wiped his long hands against the coarse sack on the desk and stood. He arched his back and stretched his arms above his head. He turned the lantern down low, but not off. It would burn itself out but he liked the light while he fell asleep, he liked knowing who and what was in his bedroom at all times.

The sheets crinkled beneath him as he collapsed into bed, curling onto his side and letting his eyes shut.

Sleep found him right away. As he slept, one hand crept up to his face and he slipped his thumb into his mouth—a habit he had developed as a toddler, one that resurfaced after his mother's death. He barely noticed the metallic taste of blood still left on his hand. He would wash in the morning, anyhow.

On the dimly-lit desk rested the remains of the one-year-old rabbit. To anyone observing the creature's quartering, no real order could be found, but Francis had a reason for everything he did.

He'd flayed the rabbit completely open to expose its internal organs. The muscles, he carved off the bone and placed into three different bloody mounds. He had unraveled the tiny intestines and arranged the rope-like organ into the shape of a heart on the wooden desk. He'd peeled open the lungs, then used them as painting sponges and within the macabre heart he dabbed the letters F.M. + Delia. He had plucked the tiny eyeballs from the rabbit's skull and smashed them on the desk.

The wick on the lantern burned out, casting the small room into darkness. Dozens of small animals tacked up on the walls of his room stared down at Francis while he slept.

He didn't remember dreaming, only the blackness of night, and the encompassing darkness that erased each day.

***

Delia finished her Saturday morning chores and wandered off into the woods south of the house. The combine still sat dead as a stone in the wheat field. The sound of birds and the rushing of the wind greeted her. She didn't expect to see Francis that morning, but moments later he emerged from the field, right over by the combine. Delia had a fleeting, bizarre thought. *Could Francis have done something to the combine? Is he the reason it's broken?* The notion seemed silly, and she put it from her mind.

"Hey Delia!" The boy called over to her, his voice bright and happy. "That machine out there's busted up good. Looks like the bank won't get the harvest after all."

Delia looked out to the combine, as large and unmoving as a frozen mammoth, then back to Francis. *Could he have?*

"So, you wanna go fishing?"

She nodded without hesitation.

"Come on, we'll have to go to my house to get a fishing pole. It's kind of a long walk."

She didn't care how long the walk took, and happily followed him home. She counted footsteps as she went, and by the time they arrived, she estimated they'd walked a solid two miles.

The butcher's house looked like many others throughout the Michigan countryside: a two-story square with wooden lap siding. A wraparound deck connected the front and back porches, the latter piled high with tools and pieces of broken machinery. Several cars rusted in the yard.

Delia had never met anyone who owned more than one car, but none of these looked like they had been moved in a decade. The steel hunks were more lawn ornaments than vehicles.

The wooded path gave way to the crunch of dry grass underfoot. Francis moved tentatively through the yard, his head swiveling from side to side like a bird on the lookout for a hawk. Delia found herself mirroring his careful movements, nervous without reason.

A gust of wind rushed past the house with a whooshing sound. Delia looked up at the few trees around the house and noted, with confusion, that their branches remained still, undisturbed by the wind. She couldn't feel it on her skin, either. She could only hear it.

She stopped short.

Something about that sound wasn't right.

"What are you waiting for? Come on! My fishing pole is in the shed over here." Francis paused to wait for her.

She stood still, looking at the slightly battered house and listening to the strange wind rushing through her mind. Her heartbeat sped up and heat rose into her face. She scanned every window in the house and every corner of the yard, but saw nothing out of the ordinary. She listened closely, but the wind revealed no clues.

She shrugged off a series of shivers and followed Francis to the shed—barely more than a lean-to with four poles and a slanted roof overflowing with junk.

He dug around for a moment before emerging with a short rod and reel.

"We've got to catch our own bait, of course, but that's half the fun!"

"Fun? You don't need to be havin' fun! You've got chores that need doing!"

They both jumped at the sound of a voice behind them. A pale, portly man of perhaps twenty advanced toward them.

"Shit," Francis murmured.

"Yeah, shit, you shithead. What the hell are you doing out here?"

"I'm just getting the fishing pole, Larry. Gonna go catch some dinner. Just leave us be, okay?" His words were tough, but the boy's voice rose into what Delia thought was a plea.

"Leave you be.... Larry let his voice trail off. "And who's this girl my idiot brother brought over here? She looks like she ain't right in the head." His words literally spat out of his mouth.

She didn't like the way he looked at her. His pale, oily face shone like cooked pork in a frying pan. A foul smell emanated from him, and even his clothes looked filthy. His fat face had very small eyes with large pupils; so large, they made his irises look black as well.

"She's just my friend."

"Pssft, you don't have any friends, boy." Larry rocked back and forth on his feet. "And you've got chores. Ya need to clean out the killin' room; the flies are getting bad in there."

"Pa said I can do it later."

His voice rose higher, panic creeping in.

The quiet whirring of the wind Delia could only hear grew louder and more urgent. Her legs twitched. She felt like running, but she wasn't about to ditch Francis.

"You'll do it now, dammit!" Larry shouted. He reached out and grabbed Francis by the hair. "'Cause I told you to!"

"Buster!" Francis shouted.

A large, golden-colored dog came bounding around the side of the house. When he saw Francis and Larry, the dog started barking, tucked its head down, and sprinted toward them. His lips curled up over long, yellow canines.

The fat man sneered as the dog approached, but he backed up a step. Just before the dog reached them, Larry threw Francis to the ground.

Buster nuzzled Francis, and Larry spat at them both.

"I ought to bury you and that stupid dog together."

"You couldn't bury nothin'! And Pa said you ain't supposed to be drinkin' no more."

Larry's eyes flitted around a little. He turned to Delia and leaned his face close to hers.

She pulled away.

"You come back anytime you want, now. You can come see me."

As the words dripped from his mouth, Larry reached around Delia and squeezed her bottom. Then he walked away, back toward the messy back porch of the house.

Francis rubbed at his eyes. He turned away but Delia could see the redness in his face. He ruffled the fur of his dog's head and hugged it tightly. "Okay, let's go fishing."

They reached the fishing hole—only a few hundred yards from Francis's house but in the opposite direction of her home--within minutes, but she remained mindful of the distance she would have to cover later in order to get back in time for dinner. Lunch seemed hopeless at this point.

She walked behind him as they neared the little pond. In the quiet, she heard the light swooshing of her pink dress rustling around her legs. As one of only two dresses she owned, Delia washed the garment every day.

"Well, here it is," Francis said, and nodded proudly toward a two-acre watering hole ringed by trees. A gentle slope led from the tree line down to the edge of the water. It smelled of earth, and Delia heard frogs splashing amongst the thick weeds.

"I really don't catch too much in here, but it's fun anyway. Have you ever gone fishing before?"

Delia shook her head no.

First, they went to his favorite section of open earth to dig for worms.

"Just dig in there, like this," Francis said, illustrating how to find the slick little creatures. He pulled a small silver pocketknife from the back of his trousers and scooped and scraped away dirt with the little blade.

"You can just use your fingers, too, if you want."

It would be several more days before she could have a bath, so she found a short stick to scrape through the black dirt. Though entertained by the worm-gathering, she really wanted him to bring up what happened with his brother.

He didn't seem inclined to talk about it, though, and she got the impression this type of confrontation was a regular thing.

She pulled a tiny red worm from the ground and handed it to Francis.

The creature wriggled in the boy's fingers.

She watched as Francis showed her how to bait the hook and cast the line. She felt a little bad for the worm, taken from its home, impaled on a hook, and now left to dangle in the pond.

They stayed there for quite some time, catching nothing. Francis held the pole and stared over the pond. Delia watched his face and wondered about his thoughts. Content, she enjoyed the quiet time with him. He didn't pressure her to speak. He gave her the space she needed to be comfortable.

Unfortunately, the comfort did not last long. As they sat out by the pond letting the warm afternoon blossom around them, she heard a faint rushing in her head. She ignored it at first—she wasn't ready to leave. However, the sound grew louder, and the rustling wind turned into whispers, whispers about anger, about hurt. They bounced around in the walls of her mind, colliding with each other and amplifying.

Then, a high-pitched sound rode in on the wind. Francis's head snapped up, and he looked around for the source.

"Do you hear that?" he asked.

She nodded.

Then the sound came again, louder and clearer. A short, pained scream, over and over. An animal in terrible pain.

Her heart sank and her eyes moved down to Francis as she realized what the sound must be.

He realized, too, because he shot up and took off running.

She ran as well. She had to jump over the fishing pole he'd dropped, but she caught up with him in no time. Then she passed him. She needed to get there first. Why, she had no idea.

He shouted at her from behind. "Are you crazy? What are you doing? Wait for me!"

The whispers in her head screamed at her now, and she could no longer hear her own feet crunching though the underbrush as she ran. The butcher's house loomed just ahead. She could see the roof and smell the sweet stink of decaying meat.

The dog's pained cries broke through the noise in her head. She burst out of the woods and stopped dead in her tracks. Francis's back yard opened before her.

Larry, hunched over in the middle of the yard, worked at something she didn't want to think about. Then he stood and threw a stained, wooden baseball bat to the side and walked a few steps away toward the cluttered barn.

She looked at the ground where he'd knelt.

Buried up to his neck and badly broken was Francis's dog.

Buster's head hung sideways, his mouth open, tongue limp and touching the ground. Though alive, Buster's eyes stared blankly into the sky. Larry had been beating Francis's dog with a bat until his yelps turned into whimpers and now nothing at all.

Suddenly, a rattling roar started up in the barn and Larry rumbled into view on a lawn-cutting tractor.

She looked from the fat, angry man to the dog buried thirty feet away. Her breath hitched as he charged toward Buster.

Her head pounded with malicious voices. She didn't want to see this. She had to stop Francis before he saw too. She knew well what seeing death could do to a person. She turned to intercept Francis on the path, but just then he appeared at her side.

He took in the whole scene with wide, panicked eyes, then sprinted for his dog.

Larry saw him coming. With a nasty grin, he revved the engine and activated the cutting blades.

She hoped Buster didn't see it coming, that he didn't feel anything. The tractor hit and Buster's head exploded with a loud, wet *thunk-thunk-thunk*. Big golden-haired chunks of bloody dog came shooting out of the side of the tractor, along with a fine spray of blood.

She barely heard Francis screaming over the waves crashing in her own head. She pushed her hands against her temples, trying to drive out the sound with pressure, but it didn't work. She dizzied, swaying on her feet, unsure if she would faint or vomit.

The tractor ground to a halt a few feet later and Buster's decapitated neck stuck out of the ground behind it, still spurting the last ounces of blood from his body.

Francis leapt at Larry, knocking him off the tractor and tackling him. He swung his fists furiously, driving his small hands into any piece of Larry he could. His fury was magnificent, for just a small boy.

Larry threw him off easily, grabbed Francis by the back of the neck, and stuck his foot out in front of him, running Francis into it so he would fall beneath him.

Francis flailed on the ground as his brother's fists came down on him over and over. Soon, blood covered his round, dirty face.

"Stop it!" Delia screamed as she hurtled herself at Larry. Her voice—deep and loud—came out so suddenly that it startled even her.

"Stop it now!" She smashed into the side of Larry's filthy body and knocked him off balance.

The fat, greasy man fell off of his younger brother.

Francis bled onto the ground from his mouth and nose.

She advanced on Larry. "Get away from him, you piece of dirt!" She had to scream at the top of her lungs so she could hear her voice over the racket in her head.

"Why are you here? Why are you hurting him?" She stomped up to him.

Larry scooted backwards then pulled his large body back to his feet.

"Get out of here! Go to work like a real man! Everyone in town will know you're a dirt bag if you don't leave him alone."

Larry puffed his chest up and pulled his fist up high, ready to swing at Delia.

"Larry!"

Larry spun around.

The Butcher appeared—an older man, very tall with a shock of white hair on the top of his head. He wore a long, bloodstained apron over a ratty gray t-shirt. Even from a distance, Delia could see large muscles ripple through his arms, probably from years of hauling and cutting and processing huge hunks of beef and pork.

"What's the meaning of this?" the butcher demanded.

None of them spoke as he approached. His slow, deliberate gait covered the ground quickly.

The rushing in Delia's head softened as the butcher approached. The voices did not quiet, but they slowed. They stuck to the edges of her mind, still there, still audible, but motionlessly waiting as if frightened.

The butcher took it all in.

He looked at the tractor and the bloody remains of Francis's pet dog and Larry looking on with a mix of defiance and shame. "I told you not to let me catch you killin' animals that ain't food." He advanced on Larry and stood with his chest just inches away from him. "I told you when your mother died that you better not pull any more of your shit or you'd be out of this house. That woman babied you too much, and look what it did to you."

"Pa—" Larry began.

"Quiet! Clean up this mess in the yard!"

"I'll clean it up," Francis said. "He's my dog."

He turned to Francis bleeding on the lawn, then noticed Delia. She'd been screaming like a maniac, a tall girl with rough hair and a dress covered with mud and burrs from running madly through the woods. Her face wore a thin coat of Buster's blood the tractor had sprayed on her. "Who the hell is this?" The butcher asked, pointing to her.

"She's the girl from the house. The one whose father tried to kill her."

She felt a sting hearing it aloud again.

"Aye, I knew your father. He seemed like a good man to me."

She nodded. "He was."

"You're a bit of a giant, aren't you?"

She nodded again.

"I think you'd better be getting home now, don't you?"

"I'd like to stay and help Francis."

"Fine." The man cocked his head at her. "The boy doesn't have many prospects, just to let you know." The butcher turned away from them, and Larry followed behind.

Digging the dog out was a terrible business, but they got to it. Buster's bloody fur littered the lawn, along with bits of its skull. Francis couldn't speak right then, so Delia did it for him. She sang to him, "You are my sunshine," then "This Little Light of Mine," while they worked. She did not have an abundance of emotion left in her after the ordeal with her own father, so she tried to act like the people had acted with her. Lilly had sung to her at night and it had always been comforting.

They carried Buster's body to the woods and dug a proper grave for him. She told Francis about her new home while they dug the hole for Buster. She didn't know what else to talk about, and she hadn't spoken in a long time, so she just let the words spill out. She told him about the night her father tried to kill her. He slowed his digging while he listened but still didn't say anything.

At last, they had a hole big enough to slide Buster into.

She recited the "Now I Lay Me Down to Sleep" nighttime prayer. It seemed a fitting prayer for a funeral.

Francis stood looking down at the mound of dirt. The roaring that had pounded through her head during the altercation subsided.

She thought the sound must be a warning when something dangerous or malicious might strike. The sound had nearly gone, but not completely, because faintly, from Francis's direction, she heard whispers.

He looked at her and smiled, then hugged her. "Thanks for helping."

The whispers grew a little louder when Francis squeezed against her, but she refused to believe he was a threat to her. He pulled away, his eyes still burning with anger and sadness. They weren't the warm chocolate they usually were, but fiery.

The sun had traveled a great distance in the sky above by the time she noticed. She'd missed suppertime, and she'd be in trouble for sure. With her dress filthy, and her hands, face, and feet black with dirt and blood, she'd have to take a bath right away. Aunt Deb wouldn't even want her in the house looking like this. Worse, she would have to explain what happened. Perhaps her aunt would be so happy to hear Delia speaking, she wouldn't tan her hide.

Francis walked her all the way back to her house, even though it surely meant he'd miss his own dinner.

"What made you decide to talk today?"

"It just seemed like the right time. Did you like me better when I didn't talk?"

"No. I was just surprised."

She nodded. "I was a little surprised, too. Is your brother always like that?"

"Yeah. Pa says there's something not right in his head. That's why he's not supposed to drink, the doc said it makes him worse."

"That must be scary for you."

"I'm not scared." He walked a few steps before speaking again. "I try to stay away from him as much as I can."

"Don't you go to school?"

Francis shook his head. "Do you?"

"I do. Well, I will again next school year."

"Maybe I can go then, too."

"I think that would be nice. And then you wouldn't have to be around your brother so much."

He nodded. "That's a good idea. Not because I'm scared, though."

"I know. Where did your scar come from?"

He looked down. After burying the dog, he had stripped off his filthy shirt and now a long white scar that led from just below his ribcage to somewhere beneath his belly button showed.

"It was pretty stupid. I almost died."

"Tell me, please."

Francis looked embarrassed to tell about it, but he did.

"We were playing in the hay loft when I was six. Just my brother and me. That's when we still got along. We were jumping off the bales in the top loft. Then we got the idea to take the pitchfork and toss a few bales down to the ground below so we could jump from the top loft down to the bottom."

He paused and shrugged at Delia as they walked. "It was all a little confusing. My brother was trying to pick up one of the bales. It was damp, so it was heavy. I came over to help and just then, he jerked up with the pitchfork. It tore through the bale and stuck me through the gut. He was pulling so hard it ripped all the way up my side."

"Wow."

"Yeah, it was really, really bad. My mother was hysterical and my father was furious at Larry. The doc got me stitched up inside and out. Afterwards, I got a real bad fever and they didn't think I was gonna live because of the pitchfork being so dirty or something. I don't remember that part so much. I guess my brain must have been pretty hot."

Delia nodded. It made sense to her.

"After I got better, things were never the same with me and Larry. I don't know exactly what happened, but I think my father put some real bad beatings on him. They blamed him, you know, 'cause he was the older one and should have known better. There wasn't anything I could say about it. After that, as he got older, he started drinking real bad. No one wants him to work for them on account of him being so mean."

"So, you're stuck at home with him."

"That's about it. I won't always be stuck there, though. Pa says I don't have a lot of prospects 'cause I don't know how to read or anything, but someday I'm gonna get out of here."

"Me, too." Delia took his hand in hers as they walked.

When they finally reached her aunt and uncle's house, Delia expected Francis to turn away and head home, but instead, he kept ahold of her hand and walked with her up to the porch. Aunt Deb saw them coming from the kitchen, so she came out onto the porch to meet them.

She took one look at Delia, then hollered into the house for Uncle Don.

Don burst out onto the porch.

"What the hell is going on here? Why are you so late?"

He sized Francis up and down. "Why does my niece look like this, young man? You answer me now, 'cause I know your pa."

"Sir, there was an accident at my house and my dog was hit by a lawnmower. Delia helped me bury the dog, as he was my dear friend. That's why she's a mess, and that's why she's late. It's on account of me, sir."

Don thought for a moment. "All right, then. Get on out of here. I'm sure you're supposed to be home by now."

"Yes, sir. There's one more thing, though."

Deb, Don, and Delia looked at him curiously.

"I'd like your permission to be her boyfriend."

Aunt Deb gasped behind them.

"What?" Delia yelled.

Don did a double take and looked at Delia. "You spoke?"

"That's something you should be asking me," Delia continued, "not my uncle." She stared him down with such ferocity that Francis didn't say a word.

Finally, Don broke the silence. "All right, boy, time for you to go. Just be careful around my niece." He said it with a chuckle and a stern look in Francis's direction.

Francis turned and ran down the tree line. Delia looked up at Don, then hugged him around his large midsection.

"I'm sorry I was late for dinner."

The big man hugged her back for just a moment. Then he released her to be scolded by Deb.

"You missed dinner!" she hissed. "And you're filthy! Get your butt in the bathroom right this moment. You won't be done tonight until you're clean, the bathroom is clean, and the laundry is done. Everyone's laundry!"

"Yes, Aunt Deb," Delia murmured and shuffled dutifully to the bathroom. She had gotten off light and she knew it. Her own mother would have whipped her. She stripped off her ruined clothing and left it on the floor while she waited for the bathtub to fill. Dirt darkened her arms, legs, hands, and feet, but her dress left her torso pearly white. She laughed to herself at the silliness of how she looked.

Before the bath finished filling, she lowered herself down into the tub and let her head lean back while the hot water surrounded her. As she lay there, she thought about Francis and having a boyfriend and other normal things like that. She didn't know if she'd ever be able to have a normal life anymore.

She silently scolded herself for letting her emotions get out of control that day. She resolved to keep them in check. Losing control only made her feel worse. Her family had gone to the afterlife and now she heard strange sounds that warned her about danger. She could never tell another person about that. She figured things couldn't get much stranger than this.

Still, she had liked the feeling of holding Francis's hand on the way home. That might not be so bad.

Besides, what harm could come of it?

Chapter 5

A sixteen-year-old woman stood on the front porch of the Grattan General Store. She'd grown tall, her hair long and blonde. Her body filled out her long dress where it should, but an awkwardness still surrounded her in the way she moved and the way she spoke. But Delia supposed that she'd always been a bit awkward, so it would follow that she'd be a bit odd the rest of her life. Right now, she navigated another piece of awkwardness, a man named Jonathan.

"Jonathan, I've told you on more than one occasion, I'm with another boy. Francis, the butcher's son. I believe you know him."

Jonathan smirked at her, standing outside the store his parents owned. He probably felt like a man of some importance in town, though ego had more to do with that than his actual standing. He had a handsome face and a strong jawline, with blonde hair combed up into a pretty wave atop his head. Smooth and dapper and very nice smelling, he did have many desirable qualities. He was small, though. He didn't have the muscles or the breadth of a farmer. His soft and delicate palms clearly showed he had never endured real labor. Not like Francis. He could certainly charm a girl, but held no interest for her.

"Francis, huh?" He leaned his slender body back against the side of the grocery store in a confident way that Delia presumed drove most of the other girls wild.

"Jonathan, why do you even bother?" she asked with a sigh. "Even if I weren't taken, you're too old for me. I'm still in school, for goodness' sake."

"Only by two years, Dee. You'll be eighteen before you know it. Besides," he added slyly, "that means I can teach you some things. Unlike that farm boy you've got now."

She sighed. She didn't know why Jonathan had the hots for her. She didn't consider herself one of the pretty girls. In fact, her tall stature made her look more awkward than anything, like a stork amongst ducks. "Really, Jonathan, calling me Dee is a little too familiar. I'm leaving now."

Before she could move, he swung his body around in front of her and blocked her path. "Come on, Dee, I'll show you how to do the good stuff." He spoke to her in a lascivious way, then ran his hand up the side of her arm.

She promptly slapped his hand away. "Jonathan!" She hissed.

Anger reared up in her belly but she calmly willed it back down. *Be still, don't ever show them how you feel.* That had become her mantra for the last few years. No matter what happened, no matter what came her way, she always tucked the emotions back inside, to be dealt with privately or forgotten. A wispy voice took shape in her mind. Quietly, as if reciting a prayer, she spoke once more. "You had better knock it off, Jonathan. My Uncle Don won't like—"

"Your uncle isn't here."

"But I am." The gravelly voice came from behind him and to the side. Francis had come upon the grocery store by way of a small path behind it. "You'd best back away from my girl."

Delia slipped away from Jonathan, knowing what would come. She was surprised it took Francis this long to meet her here; he normally didn't let her out of his sight for long.

"Or what, farm boy? What are you going to do about—"

He never got to finish his snide sentence because Francis's giant meaty fist slammed into his jaw with a loud crack.

Or perhaps the crack came from Jonathan's head slamming into the wood siding of the grocery store. Either way, he went down without a word. His thin, well-dressed body flopped into an uneven pile on the front deck of the store.

Francis rubbed his fist with his other hand and looked at Delia. His eyes burned with intensity, and, she thought, satisfaction as well. "You knew I was coming."

"Indeed, I did."

Francis's smirked, his eyes still alight with dangerous emotion.

He needs to learn to contain that, she thought disapprovingly.

Unfortunately, Jonathan's father heard the commotion. He stepped out onto the porch holding a black pistol.

"I was just defending Delia, sir. Jonathan was making unwanted advances, he had it coming."

"You just put your hands up, son. The sheriff will be here shortly."

Francis sighed and she shook her head. She reached out and touched him along his stubbly face. Her boy, nothing but a soft mess when they were together, but all fire and ice to the outside world. She sometimes worried he might actually combust without her there to calm him.

At age sixteen, he spent five nights in jail for breaking Jonathan's jaw. The judge promised a much harsher punishment should he reoffend.

For Francis, the punishment went beyond jail. His father beat him senseless.

After a week with no word, Delia snuck over to his house.

With both eyes blackened, he moved gingerly, favoring his midsection as if his ribs were broken.

"I had it coming," Francis told her.

A good deal larger than Francis, his old man took no shit but certainly knew how to deal it out.

She could only shake her head.

She supposed Francis's actions were brave and chivalrous—defending her honor like that—but to Delia it seemed like a waste of energy. All those emotions, all that frustration, not enough thought. So here he sat, broken, bruised, and looked down upon. He couldn't change Jonathan being a jerk, and now finding a job around town would be next to impossible for Francis.

Chapter 6

When the Red Cross announced they were in desperate need of Army Corps Nurses, Delia knew she'd found her ticket out of the country. For eighteen long years, she had toiled at the farm. She learned much from her parents before they passed away, then even more from Uncle Don and Aunt Deb.

She'd become an accomplished cook, able to prepare a family meal quickly and with little help. As far as household chores went, she'd mastered them all; though some of them she preferred not to do. She wouldn't miss scrubbing the tub with lye to remove the stains left by filthy children. She also worked with Uncle Don in his clinic for about an hour a day after school. As a veterinarian in the middle of farm country, some emergency or other always needed tending to. While sometimes a little off-putting—vets had to deal with an awful lot of feces—she liked being able to help the animals.

Horse births, though messy, soon became her favorite to assist with. The farmers always asked Don to come out when the mares were foaling, just in case complications arose, and Delia accompanied him many times. She was fascinated by the way new life could just literally fall into the world. The years had been tough but good to her.

Delia knew in her heart, though, that she needed something more, something better than what this vast farm country had to offer. She wanted to be successful and respectable. She needed a plan to take care of herself. No one else could do it. The Red Cross offered to train young women to join the Army Corps of Nurses, where she would then travel, probably overseas, to help with the war effort. The training would be a valuable education, and her experience working with Uncle Don made her confident she would excel. Helping humans couldn't be that much different from animals, could it?

"I don't really want you to leave."

"You're leaving as well, Francis, it won't be any different."

"Yes, but I liked the idea of you waiting for me here." His eyes looked sad and pouty, a stark contrast to his tough exterior.

"You know I need to get out of here just as badly as you do. There is no future here. We agreed on that, didn't we?"

"We did, but I'll miss you so much."

Delia brushed her hands over the buttons on his chest. He looked handsome in his army uniform.

"You know I'll miss you, too." She gave him a smile. "When the war has ended, I'll have a great career. Finding a job in the city will be easy for you. Everyone loves the soldiers."

"Except the Germans, I suppose."

"Yes, I suppose not the Germans. Well, let's take this jacket off for now and go for our walk."

Delia and Francis were alone in her bedroom, with the door open, of course. She ran her hands down the front of his crisp new army jacket, unbuttoning it as she did so. It took some effort to get it off his broad shoulders but she did, then carefully laid the jacket on her bed. With Lilly in school the house felt empty, hollow, even with Deb milling about downstairs.

Francis's eyes held a particular twinkle that Delia recognized as a sign that he wanted to kiss.

She leaned against him and planted a single, soft kiss. Her lips brushed against the rough skin of his cheek.

His big arms clamped about her waist as he came in for more, but Delia held him back.

"Wait for me on the porch. I'll be right out."

Francis sighed with disappointment, then did as she had instructed. When she heard him bang open the back door, she lifted her dress up to her waist and hooked her thumbs into her underwear. She slipped them down off her legs and stepped out. She tucked the underwear under her pillow and strode down the stairs. The extra air between her legs made her feel mischievous.

Once they were outside, Delia took Francis's hand and led them on their walk.

"How much training do you have left for the paratrooper program?"

"Two weeks. The hardest part is behind me and now I'm focusing on technique. I'm being selected for another unit as well. It's a special unit they call Rangers."

Delia nodded absently. "What do you think was the hardest part of the training?" Delia asked, and smiled as a light breeze blew up her dress. The warm wind felt nice against her bare bottom.

"The physical training was grueling, it seemed like it would never end. The running did in most of the weaker trainees. Miles and miles of it every day. You and I always ran everywhere, though, so I was more prepared than most. It wasn't nice, though, those assholes had us up in the middle of the night running, then PT'd us while everyone else ate breakfast."

"Do you think you'll be frightened? When you go to war, I mean?"

Francis thought about it for a moment. "I don't know yet. It's all just training right now. There isn't any real danger, I guess you could say. They're sending us off to some island for additional training next, but they won't say where it is or what the training will be."

Delia led Francis to their tree, a gnarled old thing that had stood for years among the wheat fields. She stopped when they reached the base and smiled.

"This was where we first met," she said. "Do you remember that day?"

"Of course. You were running through the field like the devil himself was after you."

Delia nodded.

"I'm going to climb it," she told Francis matter-of-factly. "Come up after me?"

"Really?"

"Yes, really, otherwise I would not have said it!"

Francis shrugged as if to say whatever.

Delia knew he was worried and distracted by his impending deployment to the war. She intended to distract him further.

With strong arms and her steel grip, Delia hauled herself up into the tree, clawing bare toes against the bark. She climbed up several limbs and looked down. Judging by Francis's wide eyes and open-mouth, her plan had worked. Once again beneath her, Francis stared up her dress, only this time, he saw much more.

Delia rotated up in the tree and moved her feet apart so they stood on separate branches. This spread her legs wider, and Francis got a very good look at her naked bottom, cloaked in soft blonde hair.

"You're...you're..."

"I know! I don't have any underwear on!" Delia closed her legs and climbed back down. The tree lived on a small oasis of grass in a sea of wheat fields. Aside from a few birds, they were utterly alone. Delia pulled Francis to her and kissed him on the lips. She'd been plotting this moment all day, so before she had time to back down, she spat the words out of her mouth.

"I think we should have sex now."

"Wh-what?" he sputtered, eyes wide. He tried to compose more words, but his mouth just moved around a bit, soundlessly.

"Francis, you're leaving tomorrow and so am I. We both may be in harm's way and I want to make sure that we have a chance to do this in case something happens to one of us." All true words, but she had her own selfish motives as well. She had reached the limit of what she could do to stimulate herself, and yearned for a deeper release.

Francis looked dumfounded, so Delia backed up a couple of steps. After taking one more nervous breath, she pulled her dress all the way off, the fabric sliding easily over her soft white skin. His eyes widened further, taking in her naked body. Thin and strong from years of hard work, she knew her body looked desirable. Delia scrunched up her dress then laid herself on the ground with the dress under her head as a pillow.

"Come on, now." Delia lay flat on her back, beckoning her boy. She spread her legs out wide, providing the last bit of encouragement he needed.

He frantically undid the fasteners of his pants and yanked them off. Then he stumbled to his knees and practically dove on top of her. Delia thought that, if not for instinct, he might have had trouble figuring out what to do.

"I didn't know how many parts it would have," he explained as he looked at her. His face was like that of a little boy who had seen a naughty picture for the first time, not the hard man in front of her.

She shushed him then and pulled him on top of her. She'd seen mating so many times in animals, she knew exactly how this was supposed to work.

With a little kissing, and a lot of grunting and repositioning, Francis finally got himself in. His movements were jerky at first but he learned the rhythm quickly. His strong arms pulled her tightly to him and their bodies moved as one, hard muscles and hot skin.

She found the sex awkward, sweaty, and a little painful. The pleasure made up for it. She had been craving this attention, she shouldn't have waited this long. She pulled her legs up and wrapped them around Francis as he thrust, lifting her hips, allowing him deeper penetration.

The huge wave of ecstasy she expected never came, but it felt damn good anyway, satisfying her in ways she couldn't on her own. More than anything, she enjoyed the fullness inside her, and the soft shoots of pleasure that stretched out through her core.

Francis, on the other hand, was in ecstasy. Sweat dripped from his face. His eyes were locked between her legs, watching himself connecting with her. She felt his movements increase in urgency, felt the tremble in him. He was about to come.

She had to physically push him out using her thighs and the strong muscles within her sex.

"Not inside me!" she scolded, pushing against his rippled abdominal muscles, getting him out before the baby juices flowed.

He climaxed hard, with his face red and his breathing ragged.

Delia lay still for a moment. She brushed her hand playfully over the fuzzy patch between her legs, enjoying the heat and the heightened sensations. Then she donned her dress once more and waited for Francis to collect himself.

It took a few minutes, but Francis got himself together. He took Delia in his arms, held her tightly, then kissed her hard.

Delia returned the kiss then pushed him away.

"That was nice, wasn't it?" she asked.

"Oh yes, that was fantastic!" he replied. His chest heaved as he caught his breath, and his eyes were warm and full of desperate affection.

"I'm glad you enjoyed it."

"Dee, I have something I want to ask you."

"What is it? We should probably head home soon." Adult or not, she couldn't miss dinner, most especially because this would be her last dinner with her family for a long time.

Francis fished around in his pocket, then pulled out a tiny black box. He knelt down in front of Delia.

Uh-oh

"Dee, I love you. Do you love me?"

Delia blinked once before she responded. "I do, Francis, you know that. What are you doing? Come on now."

"Then I want you to be my wife." He opened the little black box and revealed a thin gold band. "It was my mother's." He looked up at her with earnest longing.

Well, she hadn't expected that.

"Francis, are you serious right now? We're leaving, how can we get married?"

"Well, not until we get back, of course, but that will give us both something to look forward to, right? Then we can do more of *that* all the time."

Delia smiled. That sounded nice, even though she felt sore at the moment. She studied him, knowing she had to answer carefully.

Unlike her, Francis's emotions completely ruled him. In fact, he seemed totally dominated by his id, the aggressive, instinctual part of his mind that operated on drive, need, and selfish desire. But aside from her adopted sister Lilly, Francis was the only friend she'd ever known. His devotion to her was clear and resolute, and the sex had indeed been pleasurable. She hadn't been thinking about marriage yet, but she supposed it had always been inevitable. After all, marriage played a big part in her plan for a prosperous future.

"Yes, Francis, I will be your wife."

Francis beamed at her, then slid the tiny gold band onto her finger. "And you will be mine forever."

"I will wear this ring as my promise to be yours and no one else's."

She looked down at the ring for a moment.

"Does this make you happy, Francis?"

"It does, Dee!" Francis hugged her tightly again.

Delia patted his back. The ring did look nice on her finger.

"Good. Let's go back home now."

"Hey, Delia."

"Yes?" Delia asked, maybe a little too sharply.

"I'm afraid. I'm afraid of not seeing you again."

"Don't be so bothered," she told him as she took his hand and led him into the wheat field.

His warm chocolate eyes sparkled with moisture.

He is such a strange man.

"I'll be your wife when you return. You'll be a good man, I'll be a good wife, and we will be prosperous."

Why did he still look so forlorn?

"If having sex makes you worry this much, maybe we shouldn't do it again tonight."

"Tonight?" he asked excitedly. His rough face brightened immediately. "Well, I'm not worried at all, then."

"Good."

***

That night couldn't have been more different. Francis seemed to mature into his sexuality in just a few short hours. Delia still shared a room with Lilly, so a secret meeting in her house would be impossible. The same went for Francis's house, because, well, it was creepy as hell.

Their earlier adventure with sex out by the old tree woke a deep, carnal desire within Delia. She wanted it again, and she wanted to improve upon the last experience. The last time they did it, she'd felt a little detached, studying the act more than enjoying it. The passing hours found her consumed by a need for more, for a deeper pleasure. She tried touching herself several times in the interim, but could not replicate the feeling of another hot body on her, with her, inside her.

Delia gathered up two soft blankets and rolled them into a bedroll to take with her. Then, as the rest of her family slept, she snuck out into the night. Francis had told her to meet him at the edge of the woods. She crept along the damp lawn with her heart beating wildly with excitement and anticipation.

"Dee, over here," Francis whispered from just a short distance away. She found him grinning wildly.

"I found the perfect place, Dee."

Delia smiled at him and followed. While she didn't feel completely confident in his ability to find a perfect spot, she really didn't care either. She just wanted more sex. Without experiencing the fierce release of pleasure and adrenaline that Francis had earlier, her body remained tense with need.

Francis led her out into the night until they entered a small clearing of tall grasses. In the middle of the clearing they found a smoothed over, stomped down depression.

"It's a deer bed," she marveled, looking up at him. "It really is perfect, Francis."

He grinned, and she placed a long-fingered hand on his hard chest, feeling the taut muscles beneath twitching at her touch. Her hand traveled down his torso, stopping momentarily at his waistband. Then she slid down further and cupped him fully between his legs. She gave him a little squeeze, and he moaned.

Delia stepped back from him. "Off with your shirt now."

Francis crossed his arms over his torso and quickly pulled off the t-shirt. The shirt dropped to the ground and revealed his heavily-muscled body.

She smiled appreciatively and grasped one of his rippling biceps in her hand, squeezing the hard muscle. She rubbed her hand over his arm, then again across the large muscles of his chest. Delia twined her fingers in a small soft patch of curly hair between his massive pectorals. Her interest flared higher as she touched him.

"Now your turn."

Delia stepped back and, with a wicked grin, slowly undid each individual button along her full-length dress. She let the garment fall silently to the ground behind her. Delia spent many hours wishing she was one of the beautiful girls, one with a pretty face and not such an awkward, tall body. But peering through her self-consciousness, the pleased look on Francis's face gave her all the confidence she needed.

Francis grinned and advanced on her, pulling her against his hot flesh. His hard, muscled chest pressed against her small, firm breasts and they kissed, hard and deep.

Delia had never felt the emotional connection many associated with kissing, but she definitely felt her sexual desire rise. She pressed her body against him. Their tongues met and danced within their mouths. Francis reached up between them and caressed one of her breasts, and then gently pinched her nipple.

Delia couldn't take any more. A hot wave of desire spiked deep within her and she pulled back from him.

"What are you doing?" he gasped.

Delia shushed him and dropped down to her knees in front of him. Then she attacked his waistband, first pulling his belt free, then whipping open the fly of his pants and pulling them off. When she finally got his pants down, she gripped him greedily. She slid her hand back and forth against him, delighted by the way he reacted to her touch.

Francis moaned above her, very ready.

"All right, lay down now," she told him softly, but in her forceful way.

Francis did as she asked, lying down on the makeshift bed.

Delia pulled his pants the rest of the way off then moved on top of him. Her body ached with longing, and she felt a pressure already building. She lowered herself down slowly on him, and her body sighed with pleasure as he slipped inside. Slowly, gently, she rocked back and forth.

With her in control, each move burned every nerve with a pleasurable fire. Even moving slowly, she began to pant, sweat rolling off her chest. She ground her body down against his, forcing him deeper and deeper inside. No matter how deep he went, she wanted more.

She rocked harder against him, swollen with a primal need she had never felt before. She leaned on Francis's hard chest, her short fingernails biting into his skin. With every move of her body, his hips came up to meet her, filling her deeply. The pressure that had already built throughout her body started to overflow, spilling sensuous heat everywhere. A powerful, electric force erupted in her core. Her arms weakened and her back arched involuntarily. Her hips bucked and she squealed in delight.

She still reeled from the orgasm but felt Francis shivering and moaning beneath her.

"Oh God, oh God," he wheezed.

Delia quickly rolled off of him and knelt down beside his legs. She grasped him in both hands and massaged him quickly. Just in time, for a moment later he erupted in an intense release of his own.

Now that, she thought, *is more like it.*

***

"It'll be lonely here while you're away."

Delia sat on her bed with Lilly. She dreaded this goodbye. Delia contained her emotions in almost every situation, but Lilly didn't live on that level of Delia's consciousness. From the very beginning, Lilly saw right through Delia's walls to the girl dwelled somewhere deeper. Lilly could always tell when Delia was hurting, and knew when she was happy, and, often times, why, even when Delia didn't know it herself.

"You've made many friends at school now," Delia said.

Lilly nodded her agreement. She had grown into a gorgeous young woman. At only twelve, her body had almost as many curves as Delia's, which in turn drew attention from all the boys at school.

"I like the new school better than the old one-room school we used to go to. It's good to be separated from the little kids. I can learn more that way." Lilly sighed and slipped her hand into Delia's. "I'll be lonely without you, Dee. You're my best friend."

As their hands connected, Lilly reached softly within her soul and slowly turned on that switch that Delia kept turned off to the world. Her adopted sister could make her feel when no one else could, not even Francis. As they sat hand in hand, Delia's eyes welled up. Their connection had always been strong and confusing. Delia didn't know why she kept herself shut down to the world. She wanted to experience fun and joy, but they just seemed beyond her reach. Not with Lilly, though. Every minute with her felt charged with emotion.

"I know. I'm really going to miss you, too," she said with tears in her eyes. Lilly made her feel good; she made everyone feel good. The tears reminded Delia of how much Lilly really meant to her.

"Do you remember when we were little, Dee, and we snuck out to stay in the woods overnight?"

An unexpected smile crept over Delia's face. "I do remember," she chuckled. "We were both so damned scared, we couldn't sleep all night!"

Lilly nodded. "We curled up against each other, pressed tight against each other's warmth."

Lilly came forward and before Delia could stop her, she placed a soft kiss on her lips. Then she looked away and leaned against her shoulder. The confusion was thick in the air between them, so they stayed silent for several minutes. Delia and Lilly leaned against each other on the bed, and Delia stroked one hand through Lilly's long brown hair.

"I don't think you'll come back here, will you?"

Delia sighed and didn't answer at first. Such a pure soul, Lilly was the last person she wanted to hurt, but she could not deceive her, so when she spoke, she did so with a heavy heart.

"No. I don't intend to return here after school. I'll be headed to the war, I think. Then, I don't know where I will go." She sighed as she spoke. She suspected Lilly already knew all of this.

"We can visit each other, though, right?"

"Of course! For now, I want you to focus on doing the best you can in school. Remember you need to prepare yourself for life every step of the way, sister. Do not just stay here." Delia tried desperately to maintain a grasp on her emotions and speak to Lilly as a wise older sister, not an unsure emotional mess.

Lilly nodded against her. "I love you, sister."

Delia pulled Lilly's head up to her own and kissed her on the cheek. "I love you too, sister. I will visit you as soon as I can."

Delia walked out of the bedroom then, bound for the city and for the Army Corps of Nurses training school. She looked back at the house as she climbed into her getaway vehicle. Lilly waved to her from the upstairs window. Delia smiled and waved back to her little sister. As she turned away from the house, tears streamed down her face. Though she'd held her emotions tightly in check most of her life, she couldn't keep them contained as she walked away from the one person she cared about more than any other.

Chapter 7

At twenty years old, Delia graduated from nursing school, and four weeks later, the Army Corps Of Nurses. As she expected, the learning came easily for her. Unlike grade school and high school, where half of her troubles had been avoiding strange social situations and managing Francis's uneven temperament, the academy offered a regimented environment of learning, instruction, and repetition.

Already accustomed to hard work and the practice of medicine from assisting Uncle Don with his veterinary practice, Delia excelled. Much of what they did at the academy was surprisingly similar to working with cows and pigs. The way skin reacted to a scalpel, the type of sutures used to close a wound, and even the calming mannerisms needed to keep patients at ease were no different than when she'd had to coax an angry bull into submission. Giving injections was something so elementary for her that the instructors had her helping other students on the first day.

Many times, she received compliments from her instructors, especially on her composure and cool headedness in the face of a troublesome or complicated case. The other women were squeamish and sometimes quite immature. During one exercise, the instructors unfolded a sheet to reveal a fully nude male with battle wounds on his midsection. While the other girls giggled and one young woman even shielded her eyes, Delia methodically went through her procedures. She ignored the flaccid penis in front of her and assessed the injuries in order to dress them properly without wasting any time on childish behavior.

A bull's penis is much more impressive anyway, she thought.

Some of these girls were going to have trouble in the field. But she had only one goal: to be the best nurse she could be. The best nurses would get the best recommendations to work in private offices after the war, and that would give her the respect and security she needed.

After a rushed graduation ceremony, a female instructor pulled Delia aside. Delia knew her from several of her classes as a sharp but unforgiving taskmaster.

"Nurse Jensen."

"Yes ma'am?" Delia stood still with her chin high, awaiting instruction.

"The army requires your service overseas. You and most of your graduating class will be heading to Europe right away."

"I understand. I'm ready to go wherever I'm needed." Willingness to serve in the European war campaign was one of the requirements for all nurses who accepted the army's aid in paying for nursing school. "How long do I have before I leave?"

"Less than twenty-four hours. You're leaving today, if you're able."

"I'm ready." She said the words without hesitation, but she had really hoped to go back and see Lilly one last time before leaving for the war. Her heart ached to see her sister again and to have a meal with her family. She wanted to give Uncle Don a hug and thank him for everything he had done for her. She had to think about what was best for her career, though.

"I knew you would be. There's a critical shortage of nurses right now. Even though you aren't experienced in the field, your proficiency in the classroom will more than make up for what you lack in experience."

"Thank you, ma'am."

"You're welcome." The woman paused. " I'm actually going to be joining you."

Delia startled just a bit. "Really, ma'am?"

"Yes, really, and you don't need to call me ma'am now. We're both nurses in the corps." The woman put her hand on Delia's shoulder and Delia looked over to see her smiling. The instructor's eyes were clear blue and a tight bun held long burgundy hair back away from her face. *Such a strange thing,* she thought, *to see these emotions on such a hardass instructor.*

"Nurse Jensen, you were our best student for this last session. Does that make you happy?"

Her words spread over her like honey on fresh bread. Delia smiled broadly now. "It does, ma'am. I mean—" she paused. "Ma'am, what's your name?"

The woman chuckled, a pleasant, musical sound. "My name's Alice. My friends call me Ali."

"What should I call you?"

"Call me Alice, for now, but we'll see where it goes." She smiled as she spoke.

A striking woman, Alice stood just as tall as Delia but with more feminine lines. Her tight uniform curved gracefully over her long body.

Delia wondered why she noticed Alice's physique at all; she didn't normally pay attention to people's clothing or body types.

"So, you're going to be my roomy for a while."

Roomy? The casual tone threw her. The past two years had been run with military efficiency and decorum. Delia wasn't prepared to engage in casual conversation. In fact, she'd never been good at making small talk. *I'll have to work on that.* Alice must have noticed her quizzical look, because she continued.

"The two of us are headed for the airport. We'll fly out to the East Coast, and from there we'll make the flight over the big pond. We're going to have a whole day in New York, so I was planning on getting a nice room downtown. You don't mind bunking with me for a little while, do you?"

"Well, no. No, I don't suppose so. Won't we just be shipping out with the other nurses?"

Alice had a bit of a mischievous tone when she spoke again. "I guess you could say I get special treatment because I'm an instructor, and I want you with me."

Delia still stood tall in front of her, as if she were receiving instruction in the classroom. *Why does she want me to go with her?* This seemed highly unusual, but not necessarily inappropriate either. *I've always wanted to go to the big city, anyway.* Though she didn't quite understand this new development, she knew better than to question her superior. Even if they were both nurses, Alice was also an officer. "If you want me, then you've got me."

"All right," Alice said happily. "Go pack your things, then, and we'll hit the road."

Delia nodded sharply and turned to leave.

"Oh, and Nurse Jensen?"

Delia stopped and turned back.

"Yes ma'am?"

"It'll be fun."

Fun? Heading to war? Delia offered a confused smile.

She thought she saw a hint of something mischievous in the instructor's eyes again.

"Yes, ma'am. I mean, Alice."

***

New York City held a grandeur beyond anything Delia could have imagined. The tallest buildings in her hometown of Grattan were grain silos and the large three-story barns that stood sentinel beside them. In New York, even the shortest buildings dwarfed the barns and silos of her small town. Everything towered above her, sights and sounds she had never experienced before. Her neck hurt from staring up, and she felt like her senses would overflow and everyone around her would see her for a confused bundle of wonder. Alice took her to famous boutiques where one could only view clothing with an appointment. They traveled to the top of the Empire State Building, and Delia experienced the terrifying thrill of vertigo for the first time.

The city was perfect, everything she had dreamed and then some. The people of the city were almost as impressive as the buildings; men and women dressed finely, laughing, walking the streets with confidence, the *click click* of their hard-heeled shoes echoing all around her. As she took in the amazing sights, her resolve strengthened. She wanted to be part of this world, to leave the desperate loneliness she had always felt and be one with this city of vibrant, beautiful people, far away from the farm and the fields and the biting tang of manure year-round.

She belonged here.

A pang of sadness struck her. *This is the type of place where Lilly belongs, too.* Her sister was far too bright and beautiful to be stuck back in Grattan, but in a place like New York she could shine. Guilt crept over her heart at leaving Lilly behind.

After a very busy day, Alice decided they needed to experience New York's nightlife before leaving for England in the morning. She and Delia had spent most of the evening touring the city.

Alice was vibrant. Every step she took seemed to be filled with life, while Delia's steps had always been filled with purpose. The way she carried her tall body, as if it were weightless, mesmerized Delia. Even the way her thin cigarettes darted in and out of her mouth seemed perfectly poised and effortless. Alice dragged Delia in and out of small taverns until her feet hurt.

At last, they stopped at a well-lit club where the sounds of laughter and music leaked out onto the street. When they went inside, Delia saw, to her amazement, dancing. Dancing like nothing she'd ever seen. Not the structured, choreographed movements of the country dances they had back home. This dancing lived, it breathed, wild and visceral, and the music filled Delia's heart and body with a pleasant pulsing vibration. Her sore feet ached but she couldn't stop them from trying to move with the beats.

Alice found two other women she knew from the Nurse Corps in the club. The way Alice could start up a conversation with anyone, gracefully and effortlessly, amazed Delia. She got so wrapped up in her own observations that Alice caught her completely off-guard when she grabbed her arm and hauled her out to the wood floor where a group of happy well-dressed people danced.

"Alice!" Delia squealed fearfully, "I don't want to do this! I don't know what I'm doing!" Her eyes widened and her pulse quickened. Bodies flashed by, some bumping into her, swirling around the chaotic dance floor.

Alice stilled her for a moment by grabbing both of her arms and holding her face to face.

"You just follow my lead, Nurse Jensen." Alice's voice poured out as sweet as honey. The intensity in her eyes, the determination and drive, told Delia she could trust her. So she did, following Alice's graceful form as she moved about the living dance floor.

Something startling happened as Delia pulled, pushed, and twirled about in this alien landscape: she started giggling. A wide grin stuck to her face and waves of laughter just kept coming out of her. Her deep laughter mingled with the other voices and bodies, rich and real, filled with wonder and mirth. For the first time in her life Delia didn't feel strange, didn't stand out from the crowd, she just had fun.

Alice laughed too. She pulled Delia close against her; so close, their bodies touched.

"I knew you had it in you, Nurse Jensen." Alice had a sparkle in her eyes.

"Call me Delia, Alice." Delia said, out of breath from the dancing and in awe of the effortless way Alice moved her perfect figure over the dance floor, keeping Delia close with every step.

Then they were jostled from the dance floor by one of the other nurses whom they had met there. She held three glasses full of dark amber liquid that looked strong enough to drop a grown man. She passed a glass to Alice and one to Delia.

Delia tipped hers back with no hesitation. The dark liquid went down her throat fast, burning as it sloshed into her belly.

"Oh my gosh it's strong!"

"Well, we're out here to have a good time, aren't we?"

Alice giggled. She disappeared and came back with another round. Delia's jaw and sides hurt from laughing so hard, but the second drink went down much easier. Then Alice shouted out.

"Back to the hotel, ladies!"

What? My goodness. They had been drinking hard—well, hard for Delia—but Alice and the other girls seemed no worse for the wear. In fact, Alice seemed to get more revved up by the minute.

Two tall glasses of champagne back at the hotel and Delia's mind swam. Strangely happy, Delia laughed more than ever. The four of them talked long into the night, giggling like young girls again. Alice regaled them with stories from the corps. Grown men who wet the bed at night, nurses who fainted the first time they saw an open wound. The stories, while entertaining, reminded Delia of the job just ahead.

When the champagne ran dry and the girls started complaining of sore sides from all the laughter, Alice finally sent them on their way. The two visiting nurses stumbled out of the smoky hotel room, mumbling about finding a taxi late in the night. Alice closed the door behind them then flopped onto the bed.

Alice rolled onto her back and pulled the bobby pins from her hair, letting it fall around her face.

"Oh, that feels so much better."

Alice flipped over, looked at Delia, then patted the bed next to her.

Delia came over and nearly fell off the bed trying to sit down.

Alice laughed then pulled her close and wrapped her arms around her.

"Thanks for being my friend tonight, Delia."

"You can call me Dee, that's what I like."

Alice smiled. "And you should call me Ali." Alice stroked Delia's cheek. "You're a pretty girl, Delia."

Delia stared into Alice's eyes as she lay next to her. Her head was muddled with alcohol, but she felt drawn to this closeness with Alice, it felt good. "Thanks," she said, and her eyes slid closed.

She wondered about Francis right then. He had left for the war many weeks ago. She knew because he had been able to take a short leave and come to see her at the Academy. He'd seemed hardened and well-prepared, but as always, he melted under her touch. They hadn't had much time together, Delia wouldn't skip a class and her lunch only lasted forty minutes.

She made up for the brevity of their meeting by leading Francis down a seldom-used stairwell. At the bottom, they ducked into a little cubby under the stairs. Francis's lips ambushed her and his hands slid up inside her shirt. His touch felt rough, needy, but she didn't mind.

His large hands gripped her soft body, turning Delia around so that she faced the wall. She hiked up her skirt and bent over, pressing her hands into the cinderblock.

"We don't have much time, Francis," she said, already breathing heavy in anticipation.

Francis wasted no time, and Delia moaned loudly as he slipped inside her. Gripping her slender hips,

Francis crashed into her over and over, each deep thrust filling her completely. The liaison ended just as quickly as it had started. Francis grabbed the back of her hair and pumped into her as hard as he could, yanking her head back as he did.

"Not inside me," she whispered.

Francis cried out as climaxed, pulling out just as Delia found her stride. As he let go, Delia pressed one hand to her sex, rubbing hard so she could climax too. She gasped as it hit, sliding down the wall, dizzy. Francis fell on top of her, squeezing her tightly against his clothed body.

"Don't forget your promise, Dee. You're mine now. Only mine." His voice was soft but his tone was very dark.

She turned over in his arms with her hand tracing the large muscles hidden under his shirt line. "I won't forget. But you better not forget either, Corporal Marks."

Francis gave her a crooked, little-boy grin and rose, straightening his uniform.

Delia did the same.

"I mean it, Dee," he continued, "you promised to be mine forever." His eyes seemed alight with some dark fire raging within him and the intensity made Delia shiver.

She stowed her uncertainty to calm him, placing a hand on his chest. "You have nothing to worry about." But staring into his eyes, she felt unnerved, and somewhere far off, she heard whispers.

They exchanged I love yous after that and Francis said goodbye.

His departure left her with more questions than ever, and a distressing uncertainty. She'd missed

Francis, and she'd been craving the hard, sexual release, but beyond that, she didn't know what she felt. She had told herself for years as they grew up dating that she would learn about love between a man and a woman, that she would cultivate that feeling for him so that her life plan could be completed. But after his visit, she didn't know. She was starting to believe she might never be able to love him.

That day at the academy was almost two years ago.

She had made a promise to Francis, a promise she fully intended to keep whether she loved him or not. What worried her was what she did tonight with Alice and the other nurses. She'd had real fun, and she'd felt a real freedom of spirit, something she hadn't experienced since before her parents died. What did it mean? Why hadn't she ever had this kind of fun with Francis?

It only took moments after Delia closed her eyes to fall asleep, so she didn't know if what happened next was part of a dream or not. With her eyes closed, she thought she felt Alice press a kiss against her lips. For a moment, she thought she could smell the sweet champagne and bite of nicotine on Alice's breath, but then it was gone and she slept.

Chapter 8

The war was ugly. It was a hungry, dirty beast. Francis had not showered in weeks. His company had been on the march for longer than he could remember and his feet had blisters on top of callouses. Nothing could prepare a young man for the horrors of war. The disgusting, raw human tragedies he endured every day could drive most civilians mad.

Francis and his company had come over the English Channel in icy cold boats. They landed a few miles West of Omaha Beach at a desolate place called Pointe Du Hoc. Heavy machine gun fire cut down his men before they ever left the water, and many more drowned in the frigid English Channel. Only half of the Rangers made it to shore, but the punishment didn't end there. The bedraggled men still had to scale nine-story cliffs to overtake an enemy gun position and ensure a safe landing for the allies on D-Day.

Even after taking the high ground atop the cliffs, the Rangers continued losing men to unending German assaults. Then, after days of skulking through the vast French countryside, the 5th Ranger Battalion finally found and absorbed their weary group.

Francis's unit did a great deal of reconnaissance, relaying information on Nazi movements. After a time, though, they met up with other British and American forces. They navigated slowly toward Belgium to assist in the efforts there.

Advancing steadily through small villages, they drove back the occupying Nazis. Friends came and went by the bullet, but those closest to him, Johnny and Bill, always watched each other's backs.

"Think we'll kill any Nazis today?" Bill asked in a ridiculous southern drawl.

"We kill Nazis every day, Bill. Why don't you ask something smart for once?"

"Well gee there Frankie, some of us didn't make it all the way through school like you, pretty boy. Why don't you tell us what we should talk about?"

"Women, blokes!" Johnny chimed in.

"Jesus, Johnny, we've seen the women you've got in England, or Great Britain, or whatever you call it. I wouldn't be bragging about them if I were you!"

"Come on, those ladies are nice. I like the plump bottoms on them."

"What's your take on it, Frankie?"

Francis paused thoughtfully for a moment. "Well, ain't none of 'em so nice as the one I had down on the farm, my fiancé."

Bill made a gagging noise.

"But right about now, I'd definitely take an English broad!" he finished.

"Thataboy! You may have some potential, Corporal Marks!" The Englishman patted Francis on the back. They sat in an empty coffee shop drinking bottled sodas they'd found behind the bar.

"All right, gents," Johnny said, "looks like we're moving again."

Indeed, a line of soldiers flowed past their window. "Let's go kill some Germans!"

The boys didn't have to wait long for action that morning. As they entered a small town pockmarked by bullet holes, Francis knew shit was about to go down. Abandoned streets told a story of survivors holing up in their apartments. The soldiers marched into town along the main thoroughfare. Francis and the rest of his small Ranger crew led the charge, scouting around buildings and peering into windows when they heard the Panzer IV fire.

Moments later, a 75-mm shell screamed through the air between them and crashed into a building on the west side of the street. The shop exploded and huge chucks of concrete sprayed over the scattering soldiers.

Three men went down immediately and the medics swarmed toward them.

"Hey!" Bill yelled at him.

"What?"

"It's a beautiful morning, right?" Bill laughed then drew up his Garand and propped it against a wooden cart in front of him.

The Nazis had taken this village only weeks ago and their forces were concentrated in the middle of town. The remnants of the 2nd Battalion, in addition to the 5th, steadily advanced on the Nazi position, but it would have been impossible for the Germans to see the small group of Francis's men darting in and around buildings ahead of the rest of the American forces. They were like ghosts on the wind, invisible to the enemy patrols. The Rangers slipped through enemy lines with ease.

Francis and his crew of six, which included his two good friends, infiltrated the Nazi line. Besides the Panzer tank, there was only a small Nazi force visible.

Then the crew came across two cleverly camouflaged machine gun nests at diagonals across the largest intersection in town. Hidden behind stacked sandbags were Nazi gunners, waiting silently. With no other enemy forces visible, it was clear to Francis that this was a kill spot, meant to lure the American forces into thinking the Germans had retreated, then mow them down with .50 caliber machine gun fire.

With no way to warn the rest of their battalion, Francis's squad had no choice but to neutralize the threat themselves, otherwise the American forces would endure heavy casualties. Like shadows in the night, Francis and his crew split up and drew positions behind the enemy machine gun nests. Using a series of hand signals, Francis communicated with Bill, who then directed his group. As one, the two groups attacked.

The men first launched grenades into the two machine gun nests. Even before the grenades exploded the men were on the move, advancing on the Nazi positions. The grenades went off, sending a shower of dirt and blood up over the sandbags, then the two crews pounced, spraying heavy Thompson machine gun fire back and forth into the nests from above. Bullets riddled the few Nazi soldiers who survived the grenade blasts, their helpless bodies jerking against the hot lead. The kill spot was destroyed, but his men did not celebrate their victory. Snipers were already firing down on them, outraged by the ambush. Francis and his men sprinted back toward the allies. Francis laughed as he ran.

"Fucking A! Great job boys!"

***

Liege, Belgium

"Nurse," the doctor called to her from across the room.

Delia quickstepped her way through the hospital ward.

Doctor Roberts set down his needle driver on the silver tray beside him.

"I'm all finished up here. It's not the best closure, the abdominal muscles were shredded pretty badly, but I think this will take care of it. Could you clean this lad up and dress him?"

"Yes, doctor."

"Thanks, I'm taking a break."

The doctor left and Delia sat down with the patient, a heavyset ten-year-old with secondary blast injuries peppered throughout his abdomen. According to his friend, the boys had found an intact artillery shell and had foolishly thrown sticks and rocks at it. As one might expect, the story turned tragic when the shell exploded. However, for his proximity to the blast, the boy had actually gotten pretty lucky. Most of the lacerations were small and required only minor repairs, but one wound gaped open beneath his navel where a of piece of jagged steel had ripped through his abdominal wall, shredding intestines before breaking apart into several pieces. The doctor had to resect ten inches of intestines that were damaged beyond repair, and tie off half a dozen vessels.

As she worked, the young soldier in the adjacent bed watched her.

"He gonna be ok?" the man asked. Only days ago, he'd been in surgery himself—appendicitis of all things.

"Yes, he'll be fine, back to playing in no time I'm sure."

"Be awful to be a kid right now, don't you think, with all this shit going on?"

"Watch your language, private." Delia paused. Her mind drifted back to her own childhood and the horrors she'd seen. "Yes, children should never have to see these things."

She took some gauze, soaked it in peroxide, then mopped up the bloody mess the doctor had left on his bare belly. The boy was still sedated, but Delia cleaned quickly. She didn't want him to wake to the sight of all that blood.

After she cleaned him up, she applied several layers of gauze and tape. Though she loved being able to help the child, she counted herself lucky not to have many of them come in. Something about children, so innocent and soft, thrust into this horrific landscape of war made her heart hurt. She smiled as she finished putting the dressings on the boy.

"There you go, buddy, you're as good as new."

With all the pain and suffering she saw daily, the protective walls Delia had built around herself grew weaker.

"You're so efficient," a soft voice from behind her said.

Delia looked over her shoulder to see Alice standing there.

Alice smiled at her with one hand on her hip.

"I had good teachers," she responded flatly.

"That you did." Alice looked down the hospital wing to see that the doctor had exited; then wrapped her arms around Delia in a hug from behind.

Delia made a perfunctory effort at slapping her way.

"I'm taking you out tonight," Alice told her.

"I'm supposed to be supervising here."

"Kate told me she would stay late."

Now Delia returned Alice's mischievous smile. "Then I guess it's a date."

Alice slid one hand over Delia's.

"Stop it," she said. "I've got blood all over my hands."

Delia shooed her away and Alice waltzed off, out through the front door to smoke one of her cigarettes.

She and Alice had grown close over the last six months in Belgium, nearly inseparable actually. About the only thing they didn't share was a room. Alice made Delia feel alive. It seemed silly when she thought about it, because she had always been alive, but now everything seemed more vibrant and *real*.

Life became confusing for her once again. Engaged, working her butt off, and thousands of miles from home, she had found an amazing connection. With a woman, no less. Nothing inappropriate had really happened, yet. They held hands sometimes when they walked and Alice occasionally stayed late in her room with a glass of wine. Delia didn't know what it meant, but for the time being, she would just indulge the goodness she felt in Alice's presence.

Delia had almost made it out of the ward when the young soldier yelled for her.

"Nurse!"

"What is it, private?"

"There's something wrong with the boy. He just went all white, like a ghost."

Delia ran over. The boy was as white as his sheets. His chest wasn't moving either.

"Doctor!" she screamed.

Delia ripped off the bandage. The sutures were still in place, though his belly bulged beneath the long incision. *Shit.* She pulled out her shears and cut through the sutures. As soon as she did, blood poured out over his alabaster belly.

"Doctor, come quickly!" she screamed at the top of her lungs. *Goddammit.* The sutures holding his abdominal wall shut were ripping out. *But where's the blood coming from?* She had an idea, but hoped she was wrong.

"Doctor!" she screamed again. *Why isn't he coming?*

Delia pressed both hands to the wound. Blood oozed out around her fingers, making them slip over the boy's pale skin. She felt a faint *pop* as more sutures tore. *No!* Delia scooped up a handful of his bedsheets and pressed them against him. Blood soaked through almost immediately. The child began to moan, his eyes rolling beneath their closed lids. *Oh honey, just stay asleep, you don't want to see this.*

"What the hell is going on, Jensen? I told you to dress this boy, not remove his sutures!"

"I did dress him, then the deep muscle sutures tore. I think an artery ruptured, you have to get in there!"

The doctor pushed his hands into the open abdomen, and the color drained from his face.

"It's the abdominal aorta," he said. "It's dissected. I must've missed a piece of shrapnel, and when I shifted everything around it cut right through the artery."

"We have to get it tied; I'll get the thread!"

The doctor shook his head sadly. "I can't see anything nurse, and he's lost too much blood, it's all pooled in the abdominal cavity. There's nothing we can do for him now."

She dropped to her knees.

Shakily, the doctor rose and walked away, head down as the boy bled out.

The kid's eyes opened, and he stared blankly at the ceiling.

She began to weep, then moved up to the boy's side and draped her arm across his chest, holding him, blocking his stomach from view.

His lips turned gray and his abdomen spilled more blood over the bed and onto the floor. The boy mumbled something in French. Then his voice faded and his eyes slipped closed once more.

Delia cried. She cried long and hard, her body shaking with enormous grief, a mourning of life and innocence.

***

Francis dragged himself along a hedgerow that seemed to have no end. They had been ambushed twice on this path but still they pressed on, ever closer to the next town. Fatigue filled every part of his body. He had been in-country, fighting for months, and already he felt like a different person. So many of his friends had fallen. He despised the civilians they occasionally came across, and sneered when they came begging for food or offering their thanks. These people weren't worth it, not everything they'd had to go through.

Bill was still with him, but Johnny was not. Last week, they had been marching along another long hedgerow when a small detachment of soldiers opened fire on them from behind a civilian's woodshed. Francis didn't even hear the shot, but Johnny's head exploded next to him. An instant later, bullets swarmed like bees, burning through the men with no warning. The Germans numbered only six, likely left behind or forgotten by their company, but they managed to kill nine American soldiers and his British friend.

Now he and Bill were the last of their original company. Bill's jovial nature had given way to silence. The fire had gone out of them to fight for the cause. Now they were just trying to stay alive. Darkness quickly fell on the troops and the order came to stop for the night. After exhaustive efforts to secure their perimeter, the men dropped their gear and rested at last.

Francis and a few others made a small fire, then sat down and rested against the heavy backpacks they had carried all year. Francis pulled a notepad and a pencil out of his pack and wrote.

> *My Delia,*
> *It has been many months now, and I feel the weight of the war on my shoulders. I no longer feel happiness during the day. The landscape here is dull and bleak. The ground ahead of me rolls onward with no end, just as I fear this war will. Most of my friends are dead now, and those who are not wish they were. We don't even talk about home anymore, just the thought is too painful for most of us to bear. I miss those days when we were children, and we would walk through the field for fun, and run through the trees joyfully. Do you remember when we made love beneath that tree the day before I left? I think about that day and that night often. I miss you terribly, Dee. You are my only reason now, the only reason I keep*

picking my feet up and putting them down again. I hope that you will still want me when this is all finished. I have killed so many men that I fear I am no longer the man I was before. I do know that I love you, and I can't wait for the day when you will become my wife. I want things to be simple again, just you and me and no violence or politics to think about. I love you Dee. Please write me when you can, just a word from you would brighten my day.

Your Fiancé,
Francis

Francis tucked the letter into his pack and closed his eyes.

Gunfire suddenly erupted nearby. The company instantly gained its feet, but an instant too late. The gunfire he thought he'd heard was actually a barrage of mortars firing simultaneously. The mortars ripped through the air and exploded all around camp. The resting troops had no chance. Francis ran for the hedgerow. Explosions hurtled soldiers into the air, dead before they landed. Others blew apart where they stood, with nothing left of them but scraps too small to pin medals on. Another volley of concussive blasts sounded in the distance.

"Bill! Bill! Get over here!" Francis shouted over the chaos. "We need to get up there, now!"

Bill crawled toward Francis's position.

"Right, drop the packs and go in the shadows?"

"Yes."

Bill and Francis stripped out of their gear, keeping only their rifles and side arms. The second volley of mortars hit and more of their comrades died. Soldiers were strewn about the camp. Order had collapsed; the

Lieutenant had been killed and with the NCOs scattered throughout the camp, the men didn't know who to listen to.

Bill and Francis set off into the darkness. No moon shone above, but hundreds of yards ahead, he saw tiny flashes as the mortars fired again. He and Bill ran along the hedgerow. Invisible to both sides, the two men covered the distance in only minutes.

The mortars had been set up in someone's side yard. Warm light emanated from inside the house, the residents probably enjoying the show, Francis thought. He and Bill knew what to do without speaking and they made a wide circle around and behind the line of mortars. Many soldiers gathered around the launchers, smoking cigarettes and laughing amongst themselves. Francis counted twenty-five men, illuminated by their cigarettes and the flashes of their mortars.

"Shit," he murmured as he and Bill hunkered down behind the side of the house.

"There's no time to dick around, we just have to get it done."

Francis nodded. "Geronimo style?"

"Yeah buddy. Only you stay back here. You're a better shot with the Garand and I'll need you to take out as many as you can."

Francis understood. He'd always been a decent shot, and though the Garand had only iron sights, its accuracy couldn't be matched amongst semi-automatic rifles. "All right, let's do it. Hit 'em with the grenades first, then start running at them and they won't have any idea what's coming."

"Goddamn Nazi pricks."

Francis had two grenades and Bill had one. They coordinated the first throw and landed both grenades directly in the midst of the mortars. They went off with a spectacular explosion of light, then Francis tossed the next grenade into the air. The moment it exploded, taking out three German soldiers, Bill began his 'Geronimo' charge.

He sprinted directly at the group of men, who were only thirty or so yards away. As he ran, Bill fired his rifle into the group. The soldiers fell and writhed in the smoky night air.

Francis trained his own weapon on one soldier and pulled the trigger. He went down. Several more dropped under his aim.

The line of soldiers broke, their mortars successfully disabled. Only a dozen Germans remained, but he and Bill had no intention of letting them escape. Bill had run out of rifle ammo so he chased down two fleeing Nazis with his handgun out, screaming madly as he fired. He got the first one, and Francis took out the second with his rifle.

"Around the house, Frankie!" Bill waved at him to double back. Francis did so, crouching down and moving slowly through the dark. Sure enough, a second later another soldier came barreling around the house, probably searching for Francis, but ate a face full of bullets instead.

Bill kept yelling out in front of the house. Francis shook his head. *He's a fucking madman.* Francis actually felt better now, though. They needed this mad release of anxious energy, and if it came at the expense of these murdering Nazi bastards, then so much the better. Francis crept cautiously around the rest of the house. He'd almost reached the front again when he caught a glint of light from the corner of his eye. He slammed his body to the ground immediately, just as a bayonet thrust into the air where his face had been.

"Dirty German fucker snuck up on me," he cursed. Francis pulled out his sidearm as he fell, and when he hit the ground, he fired six rounds into the blackness where he had been standing. He heard the satisfying *thunk* of bullets striking flesh, then the sound of a man falling.

"Close but no cigar, you Nazi shit."

Francis rounded the front of the house and smiled. *A sitting duck.* A soldier stood there with his back to Francis, watching something. Then he realized the man had a long rifle trained on two figures running in the night.

"No!" Francis yelled and leaped, but not fast enough. The man squeezed off a shot and one figure abruptly stopped running in the distance. Francis's chest tightened and his breathing stopped for a moment. *Bill.* His teeth ground together and with a roar of pure anguish, Francis brought the butt of his handgun down on the German's cloth hat and sent him sprawling to the ground.

The man Bill had been chasing started yelling and firing in their direction. Francis didn't pay any attention. He kicked over the soldier and unloaded his full clip into the man's face.

Hot air snapped around him as blind shots from the advancing German closed in.

Francis pulled the long KA-BAR knife from its side holster and knelt down to wait for the approaching soldier.

He would gut this bastard like a pig.

When he finished, he would take care of the residents inside.

Chapter 9

Alice found Delia in bed, a complete wreck. Self-control had served her well on the farm and made her an exceptional nurse—contained, clinical, and efficient. That control gave her strength and abilities beyond many of her colleagues. Now it failed, and Delia felt like she had nothing left.

Alice must have jimmied her door open, because one minute Delia lay alone, curled in the fetal position with nothing but her nightshirt on, and the next Alice snuggled up behind her, with a long arm draped over her, holding her tightly.

"I know there was nothing I could do, Ali," Delia said, very softly, "but it hurts just the same."

Alice said nothing, only held on. Delia felt her Alice's vibrating against her, and heard the muted sound of Alice's humming. The tune soothed her like a lullaby. Delia intertwined her fingers with Alice's as they lay together. She took Alice's offered warmth and something far greater: comfort. She drifted to sleep with the afternoon sun still in the sky and Alice tightly holding her. Delia woke alone, but with a delicious smell in the air.

A moment later, Alice came into the bedroom with two cups of coffee. She sat delicately on the side of her bed, smiling as she offered Delia a cup, which gratefully accepted.

"So, I'm still taking you out tonight."

Delia started to protest, but Alice stilled her with a stern look. "You need to get away from here for a bit, and so do I. Fresh air will do us good."

Delia shook her head and sighed.

"There's more than one way to honor the dead, Delia. We can celebrate their lives by living ours."

***

Delia would remember that night forever; not because of the tragedy that had befallen the young boy in the hospital earlier that day, but for a much more pleasant reason. She would forevermore think of that night as her and Alice's first date.

The city of Liege endured destruction and economic collapse, as much of Belgium had under the German occupation. But only a few hundred yards from the hospital, a tavern still did business. Occasionally the doctors and nurses would go down to the small bar to enjoy strong beer and chat with the locals — the few of them who spoke English anyway.

Alice took Delia to La Racine Rouillée tavern for their date. Though lit by a great many wall-mounted lanterns, the bar's interior remained dim. That suited the two young women just fine, and Alice found them a corner table set back away from the other patrons.

They ordered beer and frites, then sat back to enjoy an evening off.

"Are you sure Kate is going to be all right, watching over the ward tonight?"

"Relax, Delia, she'll be fine. The only patient that requires special attention tonight is you."

"I suppose we are just right down the road, aren't we?"

"Exactly, so if the place starts to burn down, we'll know right away."

"Not funny, Alice," she said with a scowl. She knew Alice was trying to keep the mood light, and she appreciated it.

"So, Nurse Jensen."

"Yes, Nurse Koning?"

"How do you feel about being a nurse after your time at war? Is it what you expected?"

Delia tilted her head in thought. "Aside from the tragedy today with that boy? I like being able to help people. That's not why I became a nurse, though." Delia looked down at her hands. "I learned nursing so that I could have a career when I returned home. I want to have a good life, and I thought it would be a good fit for me." Regret tinged the edge of her voice.

Alice nodded. "And now? Nursing is still a good career."

"It is, but it's also different than I expected. I thought I would be able to treat patients and move on without being any worse for the wear, but it seems like every person I see leaves a little piece of their story with me. It's distracting." Delia paused again, and again looked down at her hands. She wrung them together. "I used to be pretty awkward."

Alice raised an inquisitive eyebrow.

Two large beers arrived and the girls each took a few gulps.

"I don't really know a nice way to say it, but I didn't really have a lot of feelings about things or people. I never had much empathy, I guess. That's why I thought I could do this job so well."

"It's tough to remain detached when you see the people every day, isn't it?"

"It is, and I don't think I want to be so cold anymore. But, I'm scared of all these new feelings I'm having." Her eyes briefly flitted up to Alice's.

"I feel like there might be something else out there for me too, like I need to do something more."

Alice listened quietly.

"You see, before, I had a plan. I wanted to do my best and be successful, but that was it."

"That doesn't sound like a bad plan."

"Of course it isn't. But now I look around at all the people we see come and go and the lives they're living, or sometimes the lives that were cut short, and I feel like I need to do more—living. Does that sound foolish?"

Alice shook her head slowly as she stared at Delia. A cute smile played at her lips. "I think I know what you mean."

Alice leaned over the table and grabbed Delia's hands, cupping them in her own. "I'm so glad to have met you, Delia." Alice held her stare for a long moment before leaning back to let the bartender deliver their frites. The conversation lapsed as the women devoured the fried potatoes.

"I think we all need to spend more time living," Alice said, with a more serious note to her voice. "That's why I wanted to take you out tonight."

Delia curiously observed her. "So that we could live?"

Alice nodded. "I was asked to come back to the nursing school in the states a couple months ago."

"And you didn't go?"

"Well, obviously not." Alice stared intently at Delia whilst contemplating her next words. "I stayed here because I want to be close to you."

Delia blushed without knowing why. "You like me that much?"

Alice leaned closer. "I like you the most." Her hand came up to softly caress Delia's cheek, which caused her to blush further.

The bartender returned and cleared his throat.

Delia's face flushed again, this time from embarrassment, but Alice remained composed.

"Yes?"

The bartender pointed to their mostly empty beer glasses. "More?" he asked.

Delia smiled and nodded to him. "Yes, please."

Alice did not lean away from her, but kept staring at Delia in a way that made her feel both intimidated and beautiful all at once.

"I've had a lot of boyfriends, Dee. I've had a lot of experience with what those boys call love."

Delia shifted uncomfortably in her seat as Alice mentioned her former boyfriends.

Alice's voice cracked a little when she spoke next. "I never felt anything with them like I feel when I'm near you."

The air between them thickened. Alice had revealed her feelings at last. She sat so rigidly, like she'd braced herself for anything that might happen next.

Delia had been holding her breath, and as she let it out slowly, a sincere and grateful smile played over her lips.

"I'm glad you stayed, Ali."

***

When Delia woke, her mind and body seemed weighted down. The beer had been more potent than she expected last night. Her apartment was still dim; morning had not quite taken the night from the sky. She rolled over on her side to see Alice lying next to her.

Alice? She hadn't remembered Alice staying the night, much less in her bed, but here she was.

She lifted the sheet to peek at Alice.

Alice wore only a bra and thin, shiny panties. Her tall body stretched out over the bed, a sea of creamy white skin on white linens. Her body looked fit and firm, but not hard and muscular like Delia's. She looked soft, touchable.

Delia's eyes soaked in Alice's body and a warm sensation sprung from deep within her.

What is this?

She had never looked at another woman this way. She knew lust, had felt lust, but had never felt…whatever this feeling was. Hesitantly, but excitedly, Delia reached out and brushed against the skin of Alice's stomach with her fingertips.

The soft skin tensed.

Delia smiled. *What am I doing?*

Alice's creamy body called to her, and she felt compelled to answer.

Then she did something that shocked even her. She ducked her head beneath the sheet and slid up close to Alice, pressing her face against the deliciously soft skin.

She smelled like clean laundry.

She longingly inhaled Alice's scent, closing eyes as she did. Her body lit up with excitement at the feel of her best friend pressed close to her. Her nerves came alive and praised the contact with more silky ribbons of pleasure wrapping deep down inside her.

With trembling lips, she kissed Alice. She didn't know what she was doing at first or why, but when her lips made contact with that warm flesh, her heart raced and her chest hitched with emotion. She squeezed Alice close around the middle and kissed her lower abdomen again. Her fingers kneaded the soft skin, like a cat finally getting the attention she deserved. Her thighs squeezed against one another, causing her sex to cry out for attention.

This is not proper! Her mind shouted at her, but reason had abandoned her now. Her tongue darted out for just a moment and dabbed against Alice's skin, tasting a forbidden fruit and finding it all the more irresistible.

Delia sighed deeply, trying to expel some of the static energy coursing through her. She had never felt like this before, not even with Francis that night before they left. They had simply had sex. They had done it hard and it was good and satisfying, but this was electrifying, as if the very air in the room had come alive with some unseen current and Delia rode it. This wholly different kind of intimacy intoxicated and consumed her, and Delia didn't quite know what to do with the feelings.

Alice's breathing changed and Delia lifted her head up to see Alice looking down at her.

"I'm sorry," Delia whispered. "I—I don't know what I was doing."

"Come up here," Alice whispered in reply. Even in the darkness of her room, she could see the smile on Alice's face.

"I'm so sorry."

She lay face to face with her body alongside Alice's.

Alice took her face and pulled her close. Then she kissed her.

She stiffened in her arms, but Alice continued, softly brushing her lips over Delia's. Delia inhaled every bit of her. Tremors silently shook her. *This is wrong, this is immoral.* Everything she'd ever been taught, everything she knew, argued against this moment, and for just an instant, Delia pulled away from Alice.

The moment she did, the moment Alice's soft touch left her mouth, an emptiness flooded through Delia, a pit in her heart with no end opened.

Alice breathed hard, and Delia felt her trembling, too. Did Alice feel the same way? Could she?

Delia knew no other truth than that moment, and she couldn't deny her soul when it so obviously longed for this connection.

She dove for Alice's lips with a fervor she'd never felt with Francis. She had kissed before, but never like this. Their mouths moved feverishly against each other.

Alice slid her hand up under her nightgown.

Their tongues made contact and Delia's body shuddered with pleasure. She had never felt this kind of passion. Delia deepened her kiss, opening her mouth wider and begging for Alice to reciprocate.

Alice's hand trailed up against her breast.

She held her breath, then Alice cupped her breast gently and Delia melted against the sensuous contact. A hot spring of need blossomed inside her, demanding satisfaction. Still, a little part of her brain tried to resist. Delia pulled her mouth away, panting.

Alice refused to release her. Instead, she coiled even more tightly around Delia, wrapping her arms and legs around her muscular torso. Alice trailed her fingertips in circles around Delia's breasts. Tugging lightly at her nipple, Alice sent rivulets of pleasure racing through her abdomen, down to her sex.

The sensations became overwhelming, and Alice deftly maneuvered her hand down Delia's torso, sliding under the waistband of her panties. Her fingers twirled hard circles over Delia—twice, three times—Delia squeezed her eyes tightly shut and exploded into orgasm, her entire body convulsing and contracting against the intense stimulation.

Oh my God, oh Jesus, oh my! Delia's mind reeled with the intensity of emotions running through her.

That was incredible.

No regret. No shame. Just raw, perfect pleasure. So much more intense than it had been with Francis.

Delia's chest heaved and she said nothing at first.

When she opened her eyes, Alice grinned at her.

"I love you, Delia." Her words were almost a whisper.

What?

"You do?"

"I do."

Love?

"I don't understand this."

"We don't have to understand."

"Am I a bad person?"

"I don't think so, honey."

"Can we just stay like this?"

Alice squeezed against her with her legs. "I'm not letting you go anytime soon."

"Good." Delia rested her cheek against Alice's neck. Her body tingled. *This is so naughty*, she thought. She had kissed another woman. She lay naked in bed with another woman. *I'm a freak.* She had let another woman touch her, and greatly enjoyed it! Definitely *not* proper. *What was I thinking?*

"Ali?"

"Yes, honey?"

"I love you, too." For the first time in her life, she really meant it.

Delia closed her eyes again and lay with Alice.

What would Francis think?

Nothing good. In fact, he'd be furious. She could almost hear his voice in her mind. *This isn't the normal way of things.* Worse, *You broke your promise.*

Guilt reared its nasty face within her, but she stomped it down. She didn't move away. Instead, she pulled her arms in close to her body and let Alice tightly cuddle against her. This just felt too good to be the wrong thing to do.

***

Alone in her bedroom that night, seated at a small desk in the corner, Delia set down the letter from Francis. She had only managed to read the whole thing with great difficulty. Her fiancé was not well. *Fiancé.* Francis had previously written her several letters, his spirits much higher in those. Delia had never written him back. She knew he was worried. She knew the lack of communication was distressing to him.

What can I do now? What can I say?

Hi, Honey, I slept with my instructor but I still love you?

She shook her head at the thought, not just the sheer silliness of it, but because she knew, *she knew*, she had never loved him at all. He was just another person who had inhabited her life.

Delia sighed deeply. The words she had to say were difficult and painful, but they had to be said. She couldn't live with the poison of dishonesty within her. As she set her pen to the paper, she began to cry. She had never cried over Francis, not even when he left for war. It seemed unfair to send this to him now, but also unfair for her not to send it.

She could no longer contain everything building within her. Going through some big changes had forced her to be honest with herself. Delia had real feelings for Alice—love—and Alice happily reciprocated. Though her head remained a mess, the time she spent with Alice had opened her mind up beyond the narrow boundaries she had set for herself.

She no longer saw her nursing position as a means to a financial end or just as another step in her career. She now saw it as an adventure, one during which she had met a remarkable person who made her feel more alive than she ever had before. Alice made her want to run again, to run through fields without caring, to sing loudly without fear of judgment, and to smile at silly things she'd normally not even notice.

Being close to Alice's body brought a heat into Delia's core she'd never felt before.

I am a freak. The kids at school had always said so and now, she had proof. Though some had thought her tall stature and muscles strange, they suited Alice perfectly. She *had* to write this letter, even though she knew her broken promise would crush Francis. She could not deceive herself or him.

> *My Dearest Francis,*
> *I am so sorry to hear of your troubles.*
> *The path of the soldier seems bleak, and all we*

hear in the hospital are stories of desolation. This war seems to be unending to me, and I am able to reside in the comfort of an apartment, not the hardships of the field that you must endure. I am sure the trials you face every day are arduous and may sometimes seem insurmountable, but you are very strong, you will get through them.

I think of you often, though sometimes I just do not have the words to put down on paper. I too miss the days of our youth, though in truth, my youth was an unsettling time, and I'm finding that as an adult I can really find myself. That brings me to something I need to tell you. It is something unpleasant.

Francis, I can no longer keep my promise to be your wife. My experiences here and my choices have led me down a path that is different from yours. I am afraid I have been unfaithful to you. I have broken my promise to you and I am sincerely sorry. I wish I could offer you an explanation, or better yet, not write this at all, but I have too much respect for you as a man to deceive you any longer.

Francis, please continue to be strong. You have great determination and great potential. I believe that you will make it through this war. I think that you will do great things in your life and find happiness along the way. You will always be my first everything. Thank you for your friendship.

Dee

***

Francis was a hero amongst the soldiers. For a week after the mortar attack that took twenty-eight lives, the men patted him on the back as they passed. Some even saluted him. His commanding officer told him he would likely receive a medal for his acts of uncompromising bravery and dedication.

He was not well, though.

The path had become easier now that they had left the countryside, but his mood grew darker each day. The night Bill died, Francis had carried his body back on his shoulders. He handed the body off when he returned to camp and reported the events to his superiors. That night, he couldn't sleep, and his thoughts drifted in and out of black places, places of blood and fire and anger.

Talking to himself, he'd snapped at his fellow soldiers when they interrupted. While they marched, he couldn't focus. He could only think of Delia, and getting back to the farm and the tree where they had spent so many of their childhood days. Why hadn't she written him? He'd been here for a long time now and had not received any letters from her, even though he had written her several times. Getting mail out in the field was not always possible, he knew that, but the absence of communication dragged him deeper into depression. To make things worse, winter approached, so freezing fingers and numb toes compounded the everyday misery of war.

The second week after Bill's death and several fistfights later, the other soldiers began avoiding him. He couldn't blame them. Fights erupted over foolish things, things that would not have set him off before. Now Francis had zero patience for bullshit of any kind.

As they marched closer to larger cities, the towns they passed through had cobblestone streets instead of the dirt and mud they had become accustomed to. After scouts swept through the village, the entire company set up camp for the night. That same night, a young mail carrier approached Francis and handed him a letter.

A letter from Delia. *Finally!*

His eyes widened and he excitedly patted the delivery boy on the back.

He took the letter over to a fire pit by which a few soldiers warmed their feet. They watched him warily, knowing his truculent nature. One of them, a chubby, red-faced soldier, apparently thought himself brave enough to speak. By the look of him, he knew his way around a bottle. Francis thought he looked like a pig.

"Whatcha got there, Corporal?"

The men waited in nervous anticipation.

"A letter from my girl," Francis replied. He sat down on the ground and stared at the envelope without opening it. His heart pounded with excitement.

She wrote me at last!

The date on the letter read January 12, 1945three weeks prior. He thought briefly of his Delia sitting down to write him.

"Didn't know you had a girl."

"She's my fiancé, actually. We're gonna get married soon as I get back."

Francis smiled. He hooked a finger under the flap of the envelope and carefully tore it open.

My Dearest Francis, the letter began.

***

Two soldiers entered the hospital on gurneys, through the lobby then past the tall double doors into the treatment and recovery ward. The weary gurneys rattled and their hard, plastic wheels clattered on the tile floor.

Delia and Alice waited, sitting on the edge of an elderly man's bed. He wasn't a war casualty, but rather a passerby who one of the nurses had found collapsed on the street, dehydrated and malnourished. They convinced the doctors to take him on as a patient.

"These people have been so accepting of us, it's almost our duty, isn't it?" Alice had asked the doctor, sweetening her voice and shimmying her legs this way and that so the doctor's attention stayed focused on her fantastic form.

"That's fine nurse, just as long as we have the room."

They had plenty of room. This was not a battlefield hospital, but more of a surgery and recovery unit. While they occasionally received emergency patients, most of their residents were stabilized before coming to their hospital.

Delia saw two men wheeling in the new injuries, and she hopped up to meet them at the door.

Alice stayed by her side. Looking down at the broken men, her heart sank. They were in bad shape.

After the soldiers left the two injured men, Delia picked up their paperwork.

"We have one with no name here," she said as she flipped over the papers. "We may not know his name for a while either. His jaw was destroyed. Looks like a mortar blast. They wired it shut in the hopes it would heal and he would be able to eat without a feeding tube someday. Third degree burns up and down his torso; shrapnel hit the face and was removed by the medics on site. Says he requires a catheter because—"

She paused.

"Jesus," she mumbled.

Alice looked at her questioningly.

"Says here his penis was mostly torn off by the blast."

"Good God. Looks like his girlfriend won't be too happy when he gets home." Alice chuckled a little.

"Jesus, Ali, knock it off," Delia scolded. "It's not a laughing matter."

With his face so heavily bandaged, she only saw two bruised eyes.

"He's missing several fingers and his right leg below the thigh. His ribs were destroyed."

"What about this one?" Alice said gesturing toward the second man.

"Double amputee below the hip. Artillery. He has four broken ribs. Says he suffers from severe migraines and had an infection that burned through him for three days before they cleared him to be transferred. He's been sedated for the move over."

"All right, let's put these two closer to the back door, that way if they need anything we'll know sooner."

Alice and Delia worked the quiet ward alone that morning. They made their rounds, tending to patients with no major complications. The doctor came in to see the new patients, made some adjustments to the medications they took, then catheterized the nameless soldier.

"All right, you ladies have it from here?"

"We do, sir."

Alice fed the nameless soldier using a feeding tube—a messy instrument, but the only option. He opened his swollen and bloodshot eyes.

Delia came over as Alice finished up with him.

"Need anything?" she asked.

The soldier's beat up eyes followed her.

She smiled at him. "We're going to take good care of you, soldier."

He couldn't respond, of course.

"I'm okay, hon."

"Are you sure?" Delia asked a little playfully and bumped her hip into Alice as she stuffed the used feeding tube into a bag.

"You! Are you flirting with me, Nurse Jensen?" Alice returned a playful smile.

"It's possible."

Alice glanced down the corridor then snaked a hand out to Delia's. She pulled Delia in and then leaned up, meeting Delia's mouth with her own.

Delia smiled into the kiss. It felt right, like nectar and sunshine, pleasure and excitement. A month had passed since Delia admitted to herself that she had real feelings for Alice, and that, more than anything, she desired her; more than success or respect or all the security in the world.

Alice broke away from the kiss a moment later.

"Ouch!" she said. She looked down as she was jerked sideways. Her hand had been resting against the edge of No-Name's bed.

The soldier, wrapped up in bandages, had a fierce hold on her wrist. He tried to drag her toward him.

"What are you doing?" Alice wrenched her arm out of the man's grip. "That behavior will not be tolerated!" she scolded the soldier.

Alice rubbed her arm. Several crescent shaped cuts encircled her wrists where his fingernails had dug in. Though restrained to keep him from rolling off the bed, the soldier's arm cuffs were obviously too loose. He glared at the two nurses with bloodshot eyes.

Delia shook her head at the man. "Don't you judge us, soldier. We're the ones that are going to be taking care of you, so you'd best learn to behave."

She thought she sounded tough, though it was easy to be tough with someone restrained to a bed.

Maybe they shouldn't have been flirting at work, but she'd be damned if she'd take any shit about it. As she considered the soldier's eyes, she thought she heard whispering.

Delia cocked her head to try to hear.

"What are you doing, Dee?"

"Just give me a minute." She listened carefully to the sounds. The whispers grew louder and formed angry, indecipherable words.

Then they were gone.

She shivered. She had not heard the voices for a long time, but she would not be so foolish as to forget their meaning. They had always warned her of danger.

"What's going on, Dee? It's not a big deal. It was my fault, really. I shouldn't have kissed you like that. Not in front of everybody and while we're at work. People get scared and violent when they see things they don't understand. I'm sure he was just reacting to what he saw."

"No, we need to keep an eye on him." Delia stared into the man's eyes for a moment longer.

Chapter 10

The crumpled paper danced through the air in front of the group of soldiers before landing in the burning fire pit. Francis's face froze in a state of anguish. His hands curled and uncurled slowly and mechanically. The ring of men about the fire remained quiet.

Except for Pig Face.

"What was that about, Corporal?"

Francis said nothing. His thoughts spun. Delia belonged to him. *She's mine*! What did she think she was doing? She couldn't leave him. He had to find her; find his fiancé and remind her that she belonged to him. He would also find her new lover, find him and kill him. His mind drifted to the KA-BAR at his side. *Yes, that's how I'll do it.* He'd jam the seven-inch blade into the bastard's eye until the hilt came to rest in his eye socket.

"Come on now, we've all gotten a Dear John letter before. Tell us what happened. The bitch screwing someone else while you're away?"

Francis leapt into action without thinking. In less than a second, he was off the ground and flying over the fire pit. Pig Face still wore a smug smile when Francis reached him and began pounding his fists into his face.

The large, red-faced man spattered out blood and fell to his back.

As if automated, Francis whipped out the KA-BAR, his favorite killing weapon, and plunged the knife down toward the man's throat.

Pig Face screamed as the knife rushed toward him, then a rifle stock came down on the back of Francis's head. The knife dropped from his hand, landing only inches from its target. His vision tunneled out, the fire faded to darkness, and Francis heard only echoes of the world around him.

***

"For fuck's sake, gentlemen, were you going to let him kill the man?" The young officer had a clean face and a single silver bar on his helmet. He held his rifle by its barrel.

"We didn't know what was happening, sir, he just lost it."

"Yeah. I think his girl sent him a break-up letter. Arnold over there asked him about it and the guy just flipped."

The officer nodded as he looked down at Francis. He rolled him over with his boot and looked with recognition at the small patch on his upper arm. "Ranger, huh? With whom?"

"2nd battalion," someone muttered.

The Lieutenant regarded him intently for a moment. "They came up the ropes at Point Du Hoc. True bad-asses, those men."

The soldiers in the group nodded. One of them, a young, olive-skinned man, spoke up. "Couple weeks ago, he was out beyond the lines and took out a heavily fortified mortar position on his own, saved a lot of lives. Sir."

"I remember that."

"Yeah, his friend Bill was with him. He didn't make it back, though, and now the Corporal is all fucked up in the head."

"Watch your mouth, son. If he makes it through this godforsaken war, this man will likely receive the Medal of Honor. Drag him to his tent. Someone wait there with him, and when he wakes up, inform him that if there are any further altercations of any kind involving him, I'll send MPs to detain him immediately. It doesn't matter who you are, this type of behavior cannot be tolerated."

One of the soldiers stood up and grabbed Francis by the boots.

The officer looked down at Pig Face. "I suggest you stay away from Corporal Marks, do you understand?"

Arnold nodded his understanding.

"Let this be a lesson to all of you," the Lieutenant said to them. "This man was a bona fide hero. Look at him now. This is what happens when you lose focus out here."

The Lieutenant turned to Pig Face. "And change your fucking pants. I can smell the piss on you from here."

Pig Face flushed red and looked as if he wanted to say something smart to the officer, but by the time he thought of something the Lieutenant had walked away.

***

Francis woke with a screaming headache. A young, tired-looking soldier sat beside him.

"What are you doing here?"

"Delivering a message from the Lieutenant. If there are any more problems from you, they're going to lock you up."

Francis snorted. "We're already in prison out here, aren't we? And I just lost the one thing I had to look forward to."

The soldier blankly looked at him for a moment, then spoke. "I also received a letter recently."

Francis looked away, not caring. He didn't give a shit what this peon had to say.

"The letter said that the hospital staff was sorry, but they couldn't save my wife after she gave birth to my son. She bled to death after delivering him. The boy is with my parents until I get home. If I get home."

The soldier paused as if to reflect on his own words.

"We're all dealing with shit, man. Pull it together and be the soldier everyone used to talk about."

Francis said nothing, just nodded in the young man's direction.

The soldier got up and left Francis alone in the tent.

***

Delia sat alone in the dark ward, knitting, trying to stay awake through the long hours of darkness. The patients had fallen asleep by eleven. All but the mute soldier with the bandaged face. His eyes followed whenever she walked through the ward to check on patients. She hated the feeling of being watched, the strange heaviness on her skin, as if his very gaze held weight.

Eventually, even the creepy soldier fell asleep and Delia knitted in silence. Then she heard the soft swoosh of one of the double doors opening and Alice walked in. Delia smiled at her and cocked her head curiously.

Alice quietly strode across the long corridor.

"What are you doing?" Delia whispered. "You should be sleeping, you have the early shift tomorrow."

"I know, I'll suffer in the morning."

"But why?"

"I can't stop thinking about you."

Delia blushed in the darkness.

"I just wanted to come and see you." Alice leaned in close to her face. "I wanted to smell your hair," she said as she brushed against Delia's cheek, "and I wanted to taste your lips."

Alice pressed her mouth against Delia's and she dropped her knitting.

The needles hit the ground with a muted clang. Their behavior was inappropriate, especially after the incident earlier, but she didn't care. This late at night, no one would see them.

Delia met Alice's lips with intense longing. She pulled Alice's soft body on top of hers in the chair and squeezed her tightly. Blood rushed in her ears and her heart beat madly.

Then something else perverted the sweetness of their moment, a long-ago sound that existed only within her mind. Delia heard whispering, clear and angry. She tried to block out the sound, but it filled her with its dark warning. She broke off the kiss and peered over Alice's shoulder behind them.

The bandaged soldier sat up in his bed, watching them.

Delia shivered.

He looked like a mummy over there, only partially illuminated by the light from the door.

"My God, Alice, look." Delia pointed behind her.

Alice unsaddled herself from Delia's lap. She gasped when she turned around.

"Sir!" she whispered loudly. "Lie back down, sir. You're going to tear through your new skin!"

Alice advanced toward the man but Delia held her back. The dark rushing sounds continued. Malice and hatred emanated from him. *Hatred towards us?* She didn't know, and that scared her.

"Would you like a sedative to help you rest, sir?" Delia asked.

He did not answer.

"Sitting must be very painful, but if that's what you would like to do, you may."

"What's going on with that one?" Alice mumbled.

"I don't know, but I want you to stay clear of him."

Alice made a snorting noise. "I can take care of myself, farm girl."

"I'm serious. Be careful around him."

"I am too, I know how to handle myself!"

Delia sighed. "Fine, but go away now. I don't want any more of them waking up and seeing us in a compromised position. Some of them *can* talk."

"But I like putting you in a compromised position." Alice pulled Delia tight to her and kissed her once more. "I'll be dreaming of you."

Delia blushed again in the dark, then let Alice's hand drop as she walked away. When Alice had left through the double doors, Delia stayed standing and staring at the bandaged man. The silent judgment from the wounded man reminded her that even though this felt good, her relationship with Alice would seem wrong to the rest of the world. What would she do once they left the cloistered atmosphere of the hospital?

Everything will have to be different.

What would she do when she saw Francis again?

A shiver ran through her at the thought of Francis, as she remembered him telling her that she belonged to him. *I'm not afraid of him, am I?* Delia sighed into the dark, staring at the nameless soldier. He eventually lay back down, but the angry rushing did not subside. Delia worried. About everything.

Chapter 11

Delia's relief didn't come until after the sun rose. Fortunately, medical staff lived on-site. The three-story converted apartment building looked like a parsonage and connected to the hospital by way of a narrow brick hallway, making life much easier for the doctors and nurses. She didn't pass Alice on the stairwell on the way up. She had probably overslept after her late-night foray into the hospital.

Alice got away with murder. One of the perks of being so classically beautiful, Delia figured. All the doctors admired her assets and the patients used any excuse to get her attention.

Delia considered herself an odd sort of lucky to be in this unusual relationship with her. Apart from the obvious incongruity of being with a woman instead of a man, she was perfectly happy with Alice, more than happy, really. Alice, a source of light in a bleak, depressing world, had changed her life. She greatly admired her unending kindness and rigid confidence.

Though confident in her own abilities as a nurse, Delia could admit to more than a little awkwardness out in the world. She didn't have fantastic people skills, and relating to emotions, well, that may never come easy to her. She chuckled to herself.

"Alice, if you could just give me a little of your grace, we'd be so much more even." She reached her floor and pushed through the large steel door. Exhausted, she flopped into bed as soon as she got into the apartment. Her fingers curled into the empty sheets next to her. She longed for Alice. She wanted to kiss her again and feel their bodies intertwined.

The nightmare overtook her almost immediately. A young girl again, sleeping in her family home, a gunshot rocked through the house, waking her. Her father's stomping feet on the stairs, heading for her room. Delia rolled back and forth on the bed. Sweat slicked over her body, and she moaned, fighting against the memories.

She dove under her father's legs and raced down the stairs, but she stumbled and fell into a heap at the bottom of the staircase. She lost her breath and her head struck the wood floor. She stared into the sitting room right into the eyes of her murdered mother. Mother's once hazel eyes had clouded over, lifeless.

Her mother blinked, and Delia startled with hope.

Her mouth moved open and closed, open and closed. She tried to speak, but Delia only heard a soft wheezing, a whisper.

Delia crawled elbow over elbow to her mother.

"What are you trying to tell me, Mother?"

Delia held her mother's face and the faint whispers turned into words.

"Wake up, Delia. Wake up now."

"What? I'm awake, mother. Father is after me! Come on, I'll help you up."

"No, Delia. Wake up now. She is in danger, she needs your help."

Delia stared at her mother, terribly confused, then a loud roar filled the room. It grew and grew until Delia screamed with the force of it. Suddenly, she startled awake with her legs writhing and sweat dripping off of her face.

Something was very wrong. Delia sat straight up in bed, her senses alert. Then the sounds came crashing in. Just like in her dream, her head filled with a roar of rushing voices. They crashed through her mind, echoing like waves amplified in a conch shell.

"Oh no," she whispered. Delia stumbled out of the apartment without putting her shoes on. She bolted into the connective hallway then down the stairwell. The lower she went, the louder the raucous voices became. Finally, she reached the ground floor and burst through the double doors of the hospital ward.

Though mid-day, the hospital wing stood empty except for the patients and the on-duty nurse. Delia knew right where to look. There, all the way down the hospital wing, on her knees between two beds. The mummy-wrapped soldier hung halfway out of his bed, hands around Alice's throat, strangling her. Alice scraped and gouged and shook against him, trying to pry his giant hands from her neck.

Delia sprinted through the ward. Mummy soldier noticed her immediately but did not stop. Alice's hands dropped down to the floor and her eyes rolled back in her head.

"Let her go!" Delia screamed. "Help! Help us!"

Help would never come in time, though. The man had both hands around Alice's neck.

She started turning blue as oxygen stopped circulating through her body.

When Delia reached them, she knew what she had to do. She ran up to the side of the bed and slammed a punch into the man's side, right where the wrappings covered his newly grown skin.

With his jaw still wired shut, his head snapped back in a silent scream. He dropped Alice. His body shuddered several times, then he blacked out into a heap on the bed.

Delia dove to the floor.

Alice choked and heaved and fell to her side, but she was still conscious.

"Alice! Alice, are you all right? Oh, sweetheart!" Delia said, rocking her head in her arms. "I was so scared." Delia blinked away tears as they welled up. "The doctor will be back soon, honey, then I'll take you home."

Alice nodded. She cried too. She kept trying to say something, but couldn't make the words.

Delia tried to shush her but she was adamant.

"Se-secure him," she managed to get out.

Delia understood, and lashed leather restraints to the soldier's arms. She found another set of restraining straps and secured his ankles as well.

She heard the whoosh of the door opening at the other end of the ward. "Doctor!" she yelled. "Doctor, come over here quickly!" Though she couldn't see him, she heard his shoes flapping against the tile as he ran.

"Jesus, Mary! What happened to her, nurse?"

"This man attacked her," she said, pointing to the knocked-out soldier. "He was trying to strangle her."

"Did you see it happen? Wait, why are you down here? Where are your shoes, nurse?"

"I just had a bad feeling that I needed to get down here. I came through the doors and he was on top of her with both hands."

"Is that true, Nurse Koning?"

Alice did not speak but nodded meekly.

"My God. How were you able to stop him? Did you sedate him?"

"Not really, no. I punched him in the stomach. He blacked out from the pain." Her eyes dared the doctor to reprimand her.

The doctor stared at her, then over to the soldier, blinking several times before speaking. "Well, I'm not sure what the correct response to this situation might have been. Your actions may have saved Ms. Koning, but I'm sure they will have set this man back further. However, under the circumstances, I think you did the right thing."

Delia nodded. She really didn't care if he thought she did the right thing or not. She did what she had to do to save Alice. "I'm going to take her upstairs now."

"Yes, yes that's fine," he said as though she'd asked for permission. "I'll watch the ward."

Damn right you will, she thought.

"Why were his restraints removed?" the doctor asked Alice.

Alice's voice was weak and it pained Delia to hear it, but she answered the doctor. "I— I was going to bathe him."

The doctor nodded at her.

***

Delia helped Alice up and the two of them left the young doctor to try to figure out a solution to his violent soldier problem. Delia stopped when she got Alice to the stairwell.

"Are you okay, baby?"

Alice still had tears in her eyes. "I am now. Thank God you came, Dee. I'm sorry I didn't listen to you. I should have been more careful around him."

Delia hugged her tight. "I'm so glad you're all right. I would have been lost without you."

"How did you know? About him, I mean?"

"I'll explain it to you another time, okay?"

"Okay. Don't leave me alone, Dee."

"I wasn't going to. You're staying with me now." Delia led her up the stairs and to her apartment. She brought Alice to her bedroom.

"Stand here," she told Alice, placing her next to the bed. She slowly stripped Alice's clothing off, tracing her fingers over her body, covering every curve, every line. She did it slowly, savoring the feel of her skin.

"My sweet baby," she whispered, gently caressing Alice's neck, which had a large red ring around it. It would soon turn into an obscene bruise, but not tonight. Delia kissed Alice's neck and collarbone softly. "I'm so relieved you're all right."

Alice breathed deeply as she watched Delia undress. After peeling off her skirt and top, she slid her panties down and onto the floor. She tingled with anticipation and a humming excitement began between her legs, where her soft sex waited beneath blonde curls. She took Alice in her embrace.

"I want to love you, Alice."

Alice said softly, "I kind of thought you already did?"

"Not like I'm going to love you now," she said mischievously.

As their lips touched, Delia guided them both onto her bed. She lay Alice down on the cool sheets then slid on top of her, reveling in the hot flesh beneath her. They kissed deeply, their nerves already on end from the terrifying encounter in the hospital wing. That fear they both had experienced only seemed to charge their passion further. Delia broke away from Alice's mouth and kissed the side of her neck where the skin was red and tender. She gently kissed Alice's injured skin, then moved up and took her earlobe lightly between her teeth.

"I don't really know how two girls are supposed to do this, but it feels good, doesn't it?"

Alice giggled, hoarse and awkward. She held a hand up over her mouth. "I'm sorry, it feels amazing." Alice gently raked her manicured nails across Delia's back, causing the tiny hairs there to rise in excitement.

Delia moved on, kissing along her neck again then slowly over her chest.

When she reached Alice's breasts, Delia cupped them both in her large hands and brushed her thumbs across the dark areolas. Then slowly, painfully slowly, Delia's tongue traced a path to Alice's nipples and she gently sucked one then the other. Alice writhed beneath her. Delia had never known this type of power, had never thought she was capable of the passion that coursed through her body now.

Alice let out a soft moan.

"You're being very naughty, Nurse Jensen."

Delia felt the sincerity and longing in her words. She wanted to distract Alice, and herself, from what she had gone through.

"You just stay put, Nurse Koning. I'm just getting started," Delia said with a wink, and put her mouth back on Alice's soft skin. As Delia kissed and nibbled, she let one hand slide slowly down Alice's body, way down, where it found warm flesh eagerly awaiting her. Delia's heartbeat picked up as her fingers felt the velvety soft area between Alice's legs.

"So naughty."

Chapter 12

Francis could have sunk deep into depression. His psyche could have slowly broken down, like the soles of his feet after marching hundreds of miles. That never happened, though, because he never got the chance. The troops moved quickly that morning, nearing an objective known only to his superior officers who insisted on making good time. Multiple companies, hundreds of men, moved through the rolling landscape like locusts.

At last, they topped a large hill and looked down into what he presumed was the city of Bastogne. Francis and a dozen men stayed out front on point, as always. The man next to him pulled out a set of long binoculars and scanned the city beneath them. Any advance would have to be very cautious, as the city was less than a half-mile away. The enemy, if they were down there, had the clear advantage of being able to see troop movements from almost any direction.

"Looks quiet to me," the soldier said. He passed the binoculars to Francis who perused the clusters of buildings just as the other man had.

He didn't see any unusual activity. He set the binoculars down, then stopped short and brought them back up, focusing as far into the town commons as he could. Nothing suspicious. In fact, no activity of any sort. On a Saturday afternoon, there should have been people in the streets, or out in their yards, something.

He set the binoculars down.

"Well," said the man next to him. "What do you think?"

"Tell the Lieutenant it's safe for us to advance."

"Roger." The soldier got on a large radio handset and relayed the information back to the troop.

A long, dark smile crept over Francis's face. He could almost smell the blood already. He wanted it. He needed to kill. Francis motioned to the others out front with him.

"Let's go back and get some grub. It'll take them a while to get up here anyway." The others agreed and the men headed back toward the large mass of allied soldiers a mile behind them. Once off the hill, Francis began to jog. He smiled widely, his legs springy and his heart pounding with excitement.

***

Delia woke up feeling more alive than she ever had before. Her body felt so good. She rubbed her hands across her naked torso, remembering the passion of the night before.

"Good morning, baby." Alice watched her curiously. "You sleep well?"

Delia responded by kissing her on the mouth. "I could taste you on my lips all night. It was amazing."

Alice smiled widely. "You still want me?"

"I more than want you," she said. She let her fingers trace down Alice's neck, where bruises in the shape of two large hands had formed overnight. She winced at the sight, but tried not to let Alice see.

Alice snuggled in against her neck.

Delia wondered how she had gone from being so passive only months ago to being so confident now. The passion she shared with Alice had emboldened and awakened not only the deepest parts of her libido, but had strengthened the very core of her being. She'd grown stronger, more alive, and actually optimistic about a future with her new lover. Delia decided right then that she didn't give a damn what the world or anyone else thought about them. She put her arms around Alice.

"Alice, I'm going to keep you, all right?"

Alice nodded. "Promise?"

"I promise." The door to her heart flew wide open. Alice had peeled back the protective barrier over her mind and heart, exposing all the raw nerves and dangerous emotions she had worked so hard to keep in check.   With Alice, Delia felt like she had no boundaries. Nothing could stop them from being happy. Freed from all her previous restraints, she could be anyone she wanted.

"I have some things I need to tell you about myself," Delia told her. "Things that might make you think I'm a little…strange."

"Stranger than what we did last night?"

"Well, no, probably not."

Alice laughed. Her voice still sounded strained, but joyful, too.

"My God, Dee, I came so hard, I thought I was going to pee on you!"

"Alice!" Delia gasped at her. "We are still ladies!"

"Ugh, fine. We can roll around naked together but I can't talk about pee around you?"

"That's right."

Alice rolled onto her belly and propped her head up with her hands. "All right then, out with it." With a deep, kingly voice, she commanded, "Delia, tell me your secrets." Then she burst into giggles.

Delia cleared her throat. "So, I'm just going to get right to it then, because there's no real way of telling you that won't sound insane.

"I can hear evil. Yesterday, when you were attacked, I knew something was happening. That's why I came running to find you. I could sense it, I heard it."

Delia watched Alice for a reaction.

Alice had her head cocked to the side, something she did while trying to work out a problem. She said nothing, though, so Delia continued.

"I've heard it before, several times, actually, and it's usually only when something really terrible is going to happen to me or around me. Here, at war, there's always a little bit of a tremor in the air and I can usually block that out, but there are other times it fills me so completely, I cannot shut it away."

"What does it sound like?"

"Whispers, sometimes. Other times it sounds like water rushing through a stream, or waves crashing. Sometimes it howls like wind inside my head. It's not something I asked for or anything, and I can't get rid of it." Delia sighed. "I don't want you to think I'm crazy."

Alice, with her head still cocked to the side, tried to work through that. After a moment, she nodded. "Okay. I don't exactly understand, but I don't need to. If this means you'll be able to come to my rescue again someday, then I'm fine with that."

"Really? You still want to be with me?"

Alice inched up to her a little more, and gently kissed her on the mouth. "I'm all yours."

"Then I'll always come to your rescue," Delia said with a smile.

***

The Germans didn't attack until the Allied forces were off the hill and entering the lowlands surrounding the city. Francis waited eagerly for the attack. Hundreds of American and British soldiers poured into the depression just outside the city when a thunderous roar of .50-caliber machine gun fire rained down on them from the rooftops above.

Blood and chaos ensued. Large caliber rounds sizzled through the air, cutting soldiers in half and decimating the Allied forces. All order broke down and the men deserted their positions as they ran for shelter in the city. More German soldiers eagerly greeted them. They had silently watched the Americans advance, so they knew exactly how many were coming, from what direction, and where the commanding officers stood.

Francis briefly heard the same young Lieutenant who had clocked him with the rifle barrel shouting an order before a shell exploded through his head. The Lieutenant remained standing for just a moment, then fell to a heap on the ground. *Like the headless horseman*, Francis thought. Then Francis sprinted ahead and entered the city with the first few dozen Americans. The city had turned into a slaughterhouse and strangely, or maybe not so, he felt right at home. Nazi soldiers camped out in the buildings at street level, waiting to mow them down as they came running to escape the .50-cals.

The soldiers around him looked terrified. Death and panic filled the streets. They had been caught so off-guard that these men who had marched with him for months in enemy territory had been reduced to green grunts just out of boot camp. Francis reached the doorway to a small shop and burst through.

Two German soldiers stood with rifles aimed out the windows only a few feet away from him. He grabbed one by the back of the coat and drove his knife into his chest. As the man dropped to the ground, Francis drew his sidearm and put two bullets in the Nazi next to him, who had only just realized they'd been found out. Satisfied with his work there, Francis ventured back out into the firefight, looking for his next victims.

He didn't have to wait long. A small detachment of German soldiers came running up the side street to his left. *Perfect timing*, he thought. Francis fell to one knee, raised his rifle, and fired off six shots in quick succession. Four of the soldiers went down. Francis dropped the rifle and pulled out his knife, not the standard issue army knife, but the KA-BAR. He had only used his issue for a few weeks before the tip broke off. He needed something sturdy, something he could rely on to get the job done when it really mattered.

A friend in the marines had told him about the KA-BAR—long, tough, with a matte black finish that didn't reflect light. A true warrior's weapon.

The last advancing soldier fired at him, but no one could shoot accurately while running.

Francis heaved the great knife through the air. In a split second, the foot-long weapon crossed the distance between them and found a home in the young Nazi's neck. He fell to the ground on his knees, gurgling out an incoherent prayer.

Soldiers ran helter-skelter through the streets. He didn't know how the battle was shaping up, and as he ran over the top of American and German bodies lying in the street, he found he honestly didn't care.

A machine gun boomed loudly in its staccato voice. The firefight had lasted fifteen minutes and a gray haze crept through the city from all of the gunpowder and explosions.

Francis ducked into another storefront and found a dead German soldier on the floor, shot while sniping from one of the storefront windows. Another man occupied the shop, though, behind the counter. A heavyset man in brown pants and a white apron covered with years of old stains. Rows of pastries and assorted breads lined shelves beneath the counter.

"So, you think it's okay to just let these Nazis camp out in your store and shoot us when we come down the road?" he asked the frightened man.

The man said nothing but shook his head frantically.

"No, you don't think that's okay? Then why was he in here, huh?" Francis advanced on the fat baker. The man's round body and pudgy face reminded him of his brother, his sunken black beads of his eyes so like Larry's.

The baker backed up against the wall, searching for a safe place.

"Non, non Monsieur. Je n'ai pas les aider. Je n'ai pas le choix, s'il vous plaît monsieur, je veux seulement la paix."

"Gobbledygook," Francis replied with a nasty sneer. He reached the counter that separated him from the baker. "I think you like seeing us Americans die. You think it's good sport, don't you?"

The baker glanced over his shoulder. A stairwell ran up and away just a few feet behind him.

"No," Francis said, as he palmed the hilt of his knife. "You'll never make it."

The baker ran for the stairs, but he didn't stand a chance.

Francis deftly jumped the low serving counter while pulling the KA-BAR from its sheath. The baker only made it to the first of the stairs when Francis leapt on top of him and sank the knife down between his shoulder blades.

The man shuddered and fell beneath Francis onto the stairs.

Francis grinned manically, his thirst for violence finally beginning to feel sated. The stairs creaked above him and Francis snapped to attention, pulling the knife out of the fat baker, ready to spring on whoever approached. A young, brown-haired girl in a plaid dress trembled at the top of the stairwell. Her lips quivered and tears leaked down her face.

He leapt up the stairs two at a time. The girl tried to run, but he caught her easily. He grabbed the girl by the back of the neck and slammed her into the wall of the stairwell to his left.

She cried out.

He whipped up her skirt then tore away the white panties she wore. Lust coursed through him at the sight of her tiny buttocks. He held her in place with one hand and with the other, he made to unbutton his pants. He'd only gotten the top button released, then stopped.

"I can't do this," he murmured, then released the girl and staggered back a step. She didn't move and neither did he. The lust between his legs faded as he thought back to those many terrified nights he had spent as a child. Nights he spent praying that his brother would not come in to visit with him, and the revolting horror of Larry's large body holding him down, holding his butt cheeks open. He remembered the shame he felt for days after, as he bled every time he defecated. The memories broke him free of his violent stupor.

"I—I'm sorry," he whispered to the girl.

She hid her face against the wall, her small white bottom poking out from her mussed-up skirt.

"I have to go."

He felt nothing for the girl, only confusion. He stumbled down the steps and out of the bakery, his legs moving in stiff jerks as he walked. *What have I become*? He didn't know. One thing he knew for certain: a burning, empty hate filled him, threatening to consume him.

***

Delia and Alice tried to avoid the mummy soldier as much as they could. However, his dressings needed to be changed, his catheter had to be cleaned and reinserted on occasion, and he required a bedpan. The most high-maintenance patient they had was the one they trusted the least.

Since the incident with Alice—which had yet to be explained since the soldier refused to write and couldn't speak—tensions remained high in the ward. Consequently, the army had stationed a protective detail of three soldiers at the hospital. The soldiers took shifts pacing the interior and perimeter of the building. At all times, one stone-faced soldier stood on guard in the ward that housed the 'mummy.'

Every time the mummy soldier woke, a dark rushing of angry whispers filled her head. She lived in a state of heightened anxiety.

"He's filled with so much hate," she told Alice.

"But why is it directed at you and me?"

"I don't know if it is. I think he may be angry at everyone. I just don't know. He scares me."

Alice nodded her agreement. "The doctor told me yesterday that they may be able to remove the wiring in his jaw soon."

"Good. Then we'll be able to ask him what his problem is." Delia and Alice stood shoulder to shoulder at the head of the hospital ward.

The morning sun shone through the windows and tried to brighten the mood for the rows of injured men. Delia's gaze drifted toward the back, where the mummy soldier slept. He had been here for six weeks now. Delia longed to be rid of him, and she hated the guilt that feeling brought her.

"There's definitely something wrong with him."

"Yes, besides his injuries. The hatred within him is deep and strong. I've never felt such a constant anger."

Alice gently squeezed her hand.

"I'm sorry you have to feel that all the time."

Delia smiled softly at her. "Me too. I feel like I need to know why. We have done nothing to this man…" Delia's voice trailed off on the last word. Something else rushed through her head now. Not the whispers. A thought, then a terrible fear.

"Dee, are you all right? Your face just went ghost white."

Delia turned slowly to Alice. Tears welled up in her eyes.

"Delia, my God, tell me! What is it?"

She didn't want to say. The thought, so fresh in her head, hadn't even formed into words yet. Her breathing quickened. She strode across the ward to where the mummy slept. She flipped through his chart to the page that listed the personal effects transferred over with him. Black boots, a black leather belt, and a large knife. Not helpful at all.

Alice came to stand next to her.

"You've figured something out, haven't you?"

"God, I hope not."

She knew what she had to do. Normally they would never wake the volatile man, whom they now kept restrained at all times. This had to be done, though.

"I need the shears."

"I'll get them for you," Alice said as she walked off, but not before placing a reassuring hand on Delia's shoulder.

Chapter 13

Francis walked in a daze through the cobbled streets. He saw no signs of his battalion, save for bodies on the road. He scanned over the two-story buildings on either side of the street. Frightened faces stared down from the windows above. The street emptied into a large square, and Francis paused to take stock of his location. This was the town center, but he saw no allied forces. A few scattered German soldiers scurried through side streets, running away from him.

What's going on here?

Then he heard a German voice shouting, "Verlassen sie die stadt! Artillerie kommt!"

Francis didn't know a lick of German, but he heard 'artillery'.

"Oh, shit."

The muffled boom of a howitzer in the distance sent a shockwave of fear through him.

Oh no.

The Allies bombarded the city. The first artillery shell exploded into a building a hundred yards in front of him. Deep bass thumps of Howitzers firing came faster, then so frequently that it sounded like a fireworks finale. Giant explosive shells crashed into the buildings, bringing down walls and shattering centuries old structures.

Huge craters erupted in the street and the air filled with acrid smoke and thick dust. Some of the shells soared far past him, where the Nazi forces fled from the Allied bombardment. The only thing he could do was to try to return to his troop. *Jesus, I don't have a chance in hell.*

He turned to run back in the direction of his troops but never took his first step. An 80mm artillery shell slammed into the ground next to him.

He flew backwards into the air. The blast instantly tore one leg from his body and blew off three of his fingers.

He landed with his body on fire. Unfortunately, he didn't lose consciousness immediately. As he lay on the ground, the fiery ball that consumed him cauterized the giant open stump of his thigh. Flames burned most of the skin from his torso and took two-thirds of his face. His bones shattered. Finally, in an agony that could only be properly described in Dante's Inferno, Francis slipped from consciousness.

***

Delia carefully cut away the gauze dressing from the mummy's torso, revealing a twisted mass of scar tissue beneath. Though hideous to see, Delia's training and her slightly detached nature allowed her to see them only as wounds. They did not emotionally affect her. Yet.

The soldier woke while she snipped away his bandages. He strained against his arm cuffs once, but relented when he realized he could not get to her. With his jaw still wired, no sound came from the man, but the fire raging in his eyes told Delia exactly what he thought of her.

God help her if he got his hands on her.

She peeled back the gauze from his abdominals, and snipped away the white cotton below his waist. Her stomach lurched.

Though nearly invisible through all the mangled tissue, she could see the scar. Below the man's waistband, near his groin, a nasty, jagged white scar began and traveled up before disappearing into the burnt and tangled mass of new scar tissue. The scar predated his current injuries by many years. Delia knew this because she had laid kisses upon this same scar only a few short years ago.

"Dear God," Delia gasped. Her hand flew up to her mouth and she turned away from the soldier.

Alice was there for her to lean on.

"What is it, honey?"

"Oh God, Alice, this is my Francis." Delia wept quietly into Alice's shoulder.

"Holy shit."

***

"It's over! Germany is surrendering!" The young soldier ran through the ward, hopping with excitement.

"My God, son, are you serious?"

"Yes, doctor, it's been all over the wire! The war has ended!"

The usually quiet hospital ward filled with commotion. Excited voices of the nurses and doctors mingled with exuberant cries from the wounded.

Delia hugged Alice hard.

"We can go home!" Alice exclaimed, jumping up onto her tiptoes. She took Delia's hand and looked into her eyes. "We can go home. Us."

A smile crept over Delia's face. "You still want me? Even when we go back?"

"You're stuck with me, Dee."

Delia tightly hugged her again. "I'm so glad I found you."

"Are you kidding? I found you!" They held their embrace for a little too long, looking into each other's eyes.

"Ah-hem! Nurses!" the doctor interrupted them. "There's still work to be done."

"Yes, doctor." Alice said, and strode up to him. She put her hand on his shoulder and kissed him lightly on the cheek. "We're just happy, you know?"

The tall doctor raked a hand though his greying hair. From behind thick glasses, he looked between Alice and Delia. Though his eyes were narrowed, his face softened a little. "Of course."

They found a radio and, sure enough, the news of Germany's surrender flooded the airwaves. The hall filled with relief. All except for one man.

She could feel the hateful whisperings of Francis's heart. It had been two weeks since they discovered his identity, and shame filled Delia so much she could barely stand to be near him.

She had betrayed him. She had promised him her heart, then taken it away. She took it away when he'd needed her most.

Now Francis was gone, and only this mangled, angry mess of a man remained. No love letters would come for him, and no woman would be waiting to throw her arms around him when he returned home.

Delia had broken him, and she could not put him back together.

Even as she shook hands and clapped with the patients, guilt pooled inside her. *I'm not the one who wounded him. His injuries were a product of the war.* The wounds she inflicted on him were emotionally devastating, though. *How can I make amends for this?* She knew she must atone for her transgressions, but had not even the first clue how.

That night, Alice stayed in her room again. They had spent many nights like this, alone but together in each other's arms. Sometimes they made love. Other times they just lay together. The sound of Alice's breath in her ear calmed Delia. In the drafty apartment, the warmth from their bodies kept the bed hot.

"We're leaving soon," Alice said.

"How can you know that?"

"I spoke to the head of the corps and requested that we be released back home."

Delia, lying with her back pressed against Alice, craned her neck to look at her questioningly.

"I'm sorry I didn't ask you first. I'm ready to go home, though, and I want you to be with me."

Delia nodded softly. "I'm ready to go home."

"You're still very upset about Francis, aren't you?"

"I am." Delia rolled toward Alice and tucked her face into her neck. "I feel so terrible for him."

"But you didn't do this to him, you aren't to blame."

"I know I didn't, but my heart is aching. I never used to feel things like this. I was able to keep myself together. But when I met you, when we started to be — friends, everything changed. Now I feel like my heart is right out in the open, and I can feel every joy and every pain more clearly."

"That's not a bad thing, honey."

"I know it's not a bad thing. But it's scary, and new. I feel like I'm on a roller coaster, where one minute I'm crying and the next I'm happy again. I can't seem to get a handle on myself." Delia absentmindedly stroked Alice's chest as she spoke.

"How can I help?"

"Can you just love me?"

"I can do that."

"Wait, how did you get the corps to let us go early? We're supposed to be here for another three months.

"I have a little pull in the corps, you could say."

Delia propped herself up on an elbow and studied Alice.

Alice looked back up at her with large, sweet eyes feigning innocence.

"What aren't you telling me?"

Alice sighed, then pushed herself up into a half-sitting position. She climbed on top of Delia, pressing their naked bodies together.

"I'll tell you my secret," she whispered, then dipped her head down and kissed Delia's mouth, "after you love me."

Their lips met again and again. The passion was fiery and deep, and Delia channeled the pain, fear, and worry she had felt into her hands and her mouth. She turned Alice onto her back and devoured her body, kissing and sucking, then biting. Her long, muscled arms held Alice tight against her as she bit into the soft flesh of Alice's inner thighs.

Alice moaned against her and Delia held her tighter still.

Delia gently bit Alice at the tender spot between her legs.

Alice yelped.

She pulled back but Alice grabbed the top of her head and held her in place.

"I can take it a little rough, baby," Alice gasped out. "Just as long as I know it's from love."

"Only love."

"Then love me."

Delia gave and Alice took. It was what they both needed.

At last, she let go—of everything. Afterwards, Delia fell into a deep sleep with Alice half on top of her. She had forgotten to ask Alice about her secret.

***

Delia stared down at the timepiece she held. At one time, the small gold watch had a band, but that had long since turned to dust. Her sister Lilly had given her the watch before she left for the war. She didn't know where Lilly came across the little treasure, probably on one of her many adventures into the forest.

Her sister found many treasures in the woods and the fields. The watch was her favorite. Lilly had given it to her with a sad smile, the trinket still warm from spending so much time in her pocket.

Delia rubbed her hand over the watch's smooth surface.

Lilly had been perhaps the biggest part of her recovery after the death of her mother and father.

"I miss my sister, Lilly."

Alice was helping Delia pack her belongings before they departed on the train to the airport.

"I'd like to go and visit her sometime."

Alice stopped folding a shirt, tossing it onto the bed, and came up behind Delia. She wrapped her slender arms around her from behind. "Of course we can go see her, Dee."

"Good. I don't know what my family will think of you and I being together."

"Ha! I'm pretty sure I know what my family will think, and it's not good! I don't care, either. I choose you, Dee. Don't get frightened away now, all right?"

Delia nodded her assent. "But what are we going to do? How do you know we'll find jobs? Will we live in the city? I don't want to be on a farm again. I want to leave that behind me."

"Dee, I own a cottage in Florida. That's where I'm taking you."

Delia pulled out of their embrace and looked at Alice with a stunned expression on her face.

"What do you mean you own a cottage? You're so young. How can you afford that?"

Alice sighed and dropped her arms to her side. "I never told you my secret. It's not really a secret, I guess, plenty of people know. I just don't advertise it, because then people don't look at me the same."

"Well, tell me."

"My father is a U.S. Senator. My family is wealthy," she paused, "including me. I don't need to work, Dee, and neither do you if you don't want to."

"But, then why are you doing this? The nursing, I mean?"

"I took the nursing job to get away from the house—and some other stuff too. I wanted to experience the world. I wanted to help our country and our soldiers. I wanted to get away from the same old men in my town and make a real connection with someone."

Delia looked down, embarrassed by the stories she had told Alice about her own humble upbringings.

Alice reached out and cupped Delia's face in her hands. "I found what I was looking for Delia. I found you. I'm the same person I've always been. I just don't need to worry about money. You can work anywhere you like, do anything you like, just like I can. My family has a bunch of politicians and lawyers in it. They aren't going to understand what we have together, but that doesn't matter to me."

Delia didn't speak for a long moment. When the words came, they came quietly. "I don't want you to think you need to take care of me."

"Honey," Alice said with a stern tone, "you're the one who takes care of me. Money is nothing. Money just pays for the house we live in. The important things are right here." She placed her palm on Delia's chest, over her heart.

"You're so quiet, Dee, tell me what you're thinking."

She didn't know what to think. She felt completely lost. The driving purpose she had beaten into herself all her life, to be the best so she could get a good job and have security, was no longer important. She didn't know how to process that.

"I think," Delia began hesitantly, "I think I want to go shoe shopping in Florida."

Alice stood there staring at Delia for a moment with her mouth agape. Then she burst into laughter. "Oh baby, you're going to have so many shoes!"

Chapter 14

As Delia approached, Francis's eyes burned with hate. She and the other woman had suitcases and looked to be leaving. A low growl emanated from his chest, a mixture of anger and disgust. The pain in his body was overwhelmed by rage, not only directed at Delia, but at his confinement.

They'd trapped him here like this, arms and legs strapped down to the metal rails of the hospital bed like some kind of rabid animal. A warrior, a hero for his country, and these pricks treated him like a prisoner. He sacrificed everything for these people, including his body. *It's not right*. He hadn't seen a mirror, and could only imagine the mangled state of his face. Scar tissue covered most of his torso from the explosion that burnt his skin off. When he shifted position even a little, the fresh skin covering his abdomen still complained loudly. His right hand and arm escaped injury. His left—not so lucky. From his shoulder down to his fingers, the shiny tissue twisted, with only a few mutant patches of hair poking out.

Only his thumb and forefinger remained on his left hand. The artillery blast had gone off at street level, and because of his close proximity, his left leg had been torn off at the knee. Not cleanly, either. When the explosion took apart his leg, the muscles and tendons tried to stay attached and tore up into his thigh. A doctor had told him about new advances in something called prosthetics.

"It's like a wooden leg, only much better. We can never replace your limb, but with this new prosthesis, you'll be able to wear normal pants and shoes. You'll even be able to walk."

Francis tried to take it all on an even keel, but he roiled inside. *Her fault.* She did this to him. He never would have even joined the army if not for her. Delia wanted to leave their farming community. He'd have been happy there. She pulled him away from his home, the home where he grew up, the home where his mother had taken care of him. He loved his home, and Delia took it away.

She ripped him away from everything he knew, then left him when he needed her most. She did it on purpose. She knew what it would do to him. *She tricked me. She tricked me into thinking she loved me. Then she found that…that woman.* Disgusting. How could she be with a woman? It was unnatural, the kind of thing God did not forgive. A special place in hell burned brightly for that kind of woman. *And I'm going to send her there. I'll send both of them to hell.* Not soon, though, as his injuries would keep him in this bed for weeks or months more. He would be patient.

His heart picked up pace as Delia approached. She'd avoided him ever since he tried to strangle that whore she'd been fornicating with. As his former lover came close, Francis waited for the old feelings to come back, the love he'd once felt – the lust.

They didn't.

This woman didn't even look like his Delia. She looked defiled, desecrated. She held her head high, even though she should be wallowing in her disgrace.

And when she neared, he turned away. The sight of her made him sick. Her smell washed over Francis. She smelled like soap and sex and fear.

Then she spoke. Her deep voice rolled out, smooth and defiant.

"I'm sorry this happened to you," she said.

Then she walked away. *That was it?* Her great apology for everything she had done to him? Francis fumed as Delia walked away, and the fire of rage burned through his body, charring his insides to match his exterior. He refused to forgive Delia on this day or on any day so long as he lived.

***

Delia cried as she turned away from Francis.

Alice took her hand right away.

"I'm sorry, honey," she said.

"There is nothing but hate in him."

Indeed, the rushing of whispered voices pounded angrily in her head. The sounds magnified in her mind and pressed out against her skull, until she felt like she would burst. After she'd said her piece to Francis, she thought she saw something. *It couldn't have been real*, she thought. *Could it?*

A strange cloud formed around Francis, throbbing with anger and flexing strange, ethereal muscles. The murky gray skein had fluttered to life, then dissipated just as quickly. She shook the frightening image from her head. Bad enough she heard the sounds; she didn't want to start seeing things as well. Either her imagination had run away with her, or the hatred Francis felt had grown so strong, it actually started to take shape.

Delia shuddered, and wiped a thin line of sweat from her forehead.

Alice led her from the hospital to the cab waiting out front. Normally, they would wait for some type of military transport to take them where they needed to go, but Alice had forgone any pretense of frugality now.

"We just need to get on the train and get the hell out of here, before something bad happens."

"Something worse, you mean."

"Exactly."

So many millions of young lives with so much promise had fallen victim to this war.

I'm sorry, Francis, she thought. *I really am.*

She held Alice's hand on the way to the train station. Her hands shook with anxiety, but she felt better with every block that passed, taking them further from the hospital.

"Will we have our own car?"

"Ha! I'm not that loaded, honey! There aren't any private cars on this train, anyway. The regular cars are comfortable, so we'll be fine."

"Okay," Delia responded. "I guess I'm just a little concerned about what people will think of us being together."

"Oh, I see. Well, are you ashamed to be with me?"

"I am not."

"Then let's not worry what the rest of them think about it. We may have to be a little less affectionate when we're around others, though, just in case. I'll take care of you. Look, I know you're worried. I know this wasn't the plan you had in mind. It wasn't my plan either. But how can anything that feels this right be wrong?"

"I'm sorry, Ali, I'm just feeling emotionally frayed right now. I think once we get off this continent, I'll start feeling a little more normal again."

"I'm not worried about it honey, I love you."

The cab driver observed them curiously from the rearview mirror. He said nothing, though.

Four hours passed on the train. Delia spent most of the ride watching out her window as the hills and fields rolled by. The landscape remained timeless. No matter how much people fought, or how great the scale of human tragedy, the world kept turning. The thought gave her some comfort.

"I liked being a nurse, Ali, but I think I'm ready to be done with it."

Alice patted her on the leg. "We're going to write some brand-new chapters."

***

"What's your name, soldier?" A tall, gray man sat next to Francis's bed.

The night before, doctors had unwired Francis's jaw. He couldn't stop rubbing his face. His jaw felt sore, of course, but he would take that any day. He'd eaten food through his mouth for the first time in months that morning. Only a weak chicken broth, but the taste was good, and the sensation, amazing.

Now this army captain intended to debrief him on his account of what happened the day of his injury.

"Francis Marks, sir." Speaking hurt, and the corners of Francis's eyes twitched.

"And what is your rank?"

"Corporal, sir."

"My notes state that you were in the target area of an artillery strike by our forces. Explain to me why that was."

Francis thought for a moment before he continued. Though jarring and chaotic, the events of that day replayed crystal clear in his mind. He had to tread carefully with this officer, though.

"Sir, I was pinned down by a contingent of German soldiers. I was trying to fight my way out when our forces had begun to fall back. The Germans dispersed when they heard the heavy artillery begin. I tried to make a run for it, but I was unsuccessful. An artillery shell landed twenty feet from me. I'm told I was picked up by the next company."

The man nodded. "You were with the 2nd Battalion?" he asked, his voice rising a little.

"I was."

"At Point Du Hoc?" The officer said the words with reverence.

"Yes, sir."

The man paused for a moment before continuing. "You have received recommendations from the commanding officers of the army Ranger divisions for the Distinguished Service Cross. You will also finish your career with the rank of Staff Sergeant."

"Thank you, sir."

The man stood. "Thank you, son, for your service to our country and to this world. It's men like you who led us to win this war." The older man held a hand out, which Francis shook.

"Sir, do you know if I'll be able to go home soon?"

"You're being discharged from service immediately. You will not be reassigned, on account of your injuries."

"Yes sir."

"I'll arrange for you to have transport back to the United States."

"Thank you, sir."

"One other thing, Staff Sergeant. The doctors told me there were some incidents while you were in recovery here. I was told you attacked a nurse."

Francis did not speak at first.

"A lot of young men have a hard time adjusting to life after the war."

"Sir, I woke up from a nightmare and in my sleep, I had attacked the nurse. I could not speak or I would have explained myself to her then. I'm terribly sorry about the incident."

"I understand. I served in the trenches during the Great War." The man's eyes seemed to search into his past and then snapped back to Francis. "Sometimes I have nightmares that seem more real than life. Good luck, son."

"Thank you, sir."

The captain left Francis there. Before he went, the man handed Francis a large, heavy envelope.

"These were all the personal effects they had for you."

Francis sat up on his bed in the quiet, nearly empty ward. He opened the envelope. Out slid his KA-BAR knife in its sheath. An inventory slip read: *Unknown soldier. One large black knife. One pair leather boots. One leather belt.* The boots and belt were clearly not in this envelope. He didn't care. Francis had walked four lifetimes in those boots across Europe; he never wanted to see them again.

He held the heavy knife in his palm, turning it over again and again. This blade had seen a lot of blood in the war. A thrill of excitement washed through him as he held the big weapon. Francis traced one finger over the edge of the blade. Still sharp.

"You will see action again, my friend," Francis said to the blade. "I promise." A scarred, painful smile crept over his face.

Chapter 15

The warm sun soaked into her skin as Alice napped. She and Delia had stayed up late the night before. Her lawn chair, a nylon fabric mesh, cushioned her skin just enough for her to rest without causing her back to hurt. Since their move to Florida five years ago, Alice and Delia had lived as close to a perfect existence as they could get.

Large brown sunglasses shaded her eyes from the Florida sun, and as the warmth caressed her, Alice dreamed.

***

Prohibition had ended only four years prior. Seventeen years old, tall, thin, and attractive, some folks called Alice a headstrong bitch—namely, her mother. So she left. She left her home in Lansing—their father had uprooted them after his election to the senate. Alice always hated Lansing, and leaving took much less determination then she'd expected. With her lustrous burgundy hair in long, waving curls around porcelain skin, it didn't take long to find a place that appreciated women of beauty.

She ended up in Chicago, on the arm of a former bootlegger and real-life mobster called Fast Bennie.

A hard man with a nice suit, Fast Bennie showed her the wild side of life she'd only read about in books. He had money and a shiny black car, but more than that, he had the fear and respect of every man he met. For months they played the Chicago nightlife, drinking and screwing hard, living to every excess imaginable.

As those months turned into a year, Bennie started treating her differently. The first time he hit her was in the back of his car, when Alice complained she wasn't in the mood for sex.

She thought about running right then, but Bennie had taken her out for a new dress the next day. He'd been sweet and apologetic, and she took him back with barely a reprimand. She should have followed her instincts that night in the car, before he ever brought her to the River Bottom Lounge.

Bennie had been drinking hard all evening.

He wasn't alone, Alice had been knocking back martinis for hours. She tried hard to act like a lady, but a drunken lady is no lady at all.

Alice got up to go to the ladies' room but stumbled over her own drunken feet. She sprawled out on the floor, the hem of her already short dress flying up to her waist, giving the five men drinking at the table a fine view of her unmentionables.

Bennie scowled down at her, then slowly stood up from the table. He helped Alice up off the floor, then motioned for the other guys to follow him.

He brought her to a small stockroom behind the kitchen. In the center stood a stack of pallets with several large sacks of potatoes on it.

"What are we doing in here, Bennie Baby?" Alice slurred the words.

To answer, Bennie turned her around so that she faced him, then slugged her in the face.

Alice woke bent over the sacks of potatoes, with a horrible pain between her legs. She tried to lift herself up, but large, strong hands came from in front of her and clamped down on her wrists, keeping her in place. She looked up to see their owner: Bennie.

"Baby?" she cried.

Bennie flashed his signature bright-toothed smile at her but said nothing.

The man raping her came loudly, slamming into her as he deposited his ejaculate inside. Then he pulled out with a groan.

She'd been unconscious for most of the rape, thankfully, and she thought the worst was over.

Her relief was premature.

Moments after the man pulled out, someone grabbed her hair and pulled her head up. A whiskey soaked voice growled in her ear.

"My turn now, slut."

Alice didn't know the man, just another mobster turned businessperson in a pinstriped suit. The man grabbed her exposed ass and spread the cheeks apart wide, wide enough to hurt at the seam. Then he spit on her, right between her cheeks. Alice didn't understand—until he slammed into her. She screamed, then Bennie hit her in the face. She didn't black out but felt woozy.

Alice cried while every one of Bennie's friends violated her most tender parts again and again. She cried and she swore and she begged for it to stop. She wanted to go home, where she swore to God she would never be a 'headstrong bitch' again.

She survived the gang rape with absolutely nothing left of her but a battered, hollow frame and crawled out into a waiting cab, which took her to the hospital. She received stitches in her face, and down below, along with a stern lecture from the attending nurse about putting herself in bad situations.

The next morning, she left for Michigan. She walked up to the door of her family's home with her face a black and blue mess, wearing clothes that stank of old liquor and vomit. Though her mother nursed her and cared for her, listening to her tearful stories, she never pitied Alice, at least not that she could tell. She knew that deep down her mother believed Alice had brought these bad things on herself.

The sound of the phone ringing woke Alice from her restless slumber. She opened her eyes to the bright Florida sun, never more thankful to be so far from her past. She had been crying in her sleep, and swiftly wiped away the tiny tears rolling down her face.

***

The ribs split apart as Francis slammed the large blade into them, leaving shavings of deep red meat on the counter. He picked up one half of the large beef rack and brought the knife down again. The finely-honed steel blade broke through the flesh just as it always did. He repeated this process with the other half of the ribs. He slid the finished racks to the side. He would wrap them later. Several feet away, a large pile of mostly frozen cow flesh sat, waiting for the butcher. He grimaced with each step.

It had been five years and four months since the artillery shell burned most of the skin off his body. Twisted, ugly meat replaced his once handsome face.

He had heard the children in town calling him the monster butcher. That's what he'd become, a monster — a hideous thing that no one wanted to look at or think about. The scars curved his mouth into a perpetual sneer that matched his foul temperament.

His prosthetic leg caused a pronounced limp, which only added to his odd appearance. Even though the wound had healed, the stump of his thigh ached every time he stepped down on the prosthetic, a reminder of the life he would never have. Each streak of pain that raced through him brought back memories of the war and of the fire crawling over his mangled body. When he stood for too long, the throbbing pain in his leg became unbearable. As if to insult his already mangled body, the pain reminded him of Delia, and how she'd torn his heart out.

She was meant to be his—had promised herself to him.

Memories of those terrible weeks in the hospital came rushing back, when he'd been forced to lie for weeks in horrendous pain as Delia flaunted her infidelity in front of him. It had been disgusting then and even now burned deep in his chest, a fire that raged on and forced him to keep moving, to drive him toward the goal he knew he would someday reach.

Revenge.

He would take back his fiancé. At first, he only wanted to destroy them both, but had come to realize that he needed Delia back in his life. She would love him again; he would make sure of that. He may have to dispatch the other. *Just fine by me.* Francis ran the heavy knife over the skin of his forearm. In contrast to his matte black KA-BAR, the polished steel of this blade reflected light from the sodium bulbs above him.

The reflection of his own face appeared in the blade and Francis stopped. He sneered at the mangled man.

"We will get what's ours," he said to the reflection in the blade. "We will take it back."

He hadn't found Delia. She'd never come back to town. *Hell, she may not even be in Michigan.* His heart, however, told him he would find her. He would have Delia again. God would not allow this injustice to go unpunished and He would allow Francis to be the punisher.

The grizzled reflection smiled back at him from the knife blade.

"We'll just have to be patient."

At that moment, opportunity literally knocked. Francis walked out to see who'd come calling. He greeted the man with a large, gruesome smile. *Of course. I ask, and now I shall receive.*

"Hello young man, how are you?"

"I'm fine sir, just fine."

"The business been treating you well since your father's passing?"

"I'm staying busy, quite busy. And your veterinary practice?"

"Oh, it's well. Though I'm starting to feel my age. Don't think I'll keep it up much longer."

Francis nodded to Delia's uncle Don. "It's been years, Don, I thought maybe you'd found another meat processor."

"We did, for a bit, but I thought I might stop in, see what you could do for me. The other guy was getting a bit expensive."

Francis nodded. "I appreciate that. Got a meat order for me then?"

"I do," Don said, and handed him a small piece of paper.

"I'll get on it for you shortly. Give me a day or two."

"All right son, I appreciate it." Don turned to walk away, then paused. "And thank you, Francis, for your service in the war."

Francis watched Don's big frame walk away then glanced down at his meat order. Bacon, a lot of it. Francis knew what he would do, he knew how to get Delia to come back to him. *The patch of hemlock still grows out by the pond.* Yes, Don's bacon would have some very special seasonings in it this time. Francis chuckled. Soon, he would be reunited with Delia once more. All the waiting he'd done had prepared him, mentally and physically, for this moment of triumph.

***

The call that Uncle Don had died devastated Delia. Aunt Deb was a sobbing wreck on the phone and Delia began to implode. She hung up the phone with her chest heaving and fell to the ground. *I never went back to see them.* She struggled to settle her churning stomach, her recent meal trying to make a reappearance. After a few minutes of deep breathing, Delia regained her feet and unsteadily took off in search of Alice.

Delia wandered out behind the cottage where Alice sat lounging in a chair at the edge of their small lake.

"Ali, hon."

Alice recognized the change in Delia's demeanor immediately.

"What is it, honey?" she asked, beckoning Delia to come over to her.

Delia sat sidesaddle on Alice's lap.

"My Uncle Don has died."

"Oh baby, I'm so sorry."

Little acid emotions welled up in the corners of Delia's eyes.

"Were you two very close?"

Delia nodded meekly and let the tears roll down her cheeks. She realized just how little she had spoken to Alice about her past. The fact that Alice didn't even know about Uncle Don and Aunt Deb filled Delia with even more guilt and regret for not going back to visit her childhood home.

"Uncle Don and Aunt Deb raised me after my mother and father died." Then she added curiously, "You never ask about my parents."

Alice shrugged. "You avoid them in conversation, Dee, I figured you didn't want to talk about them." Alice pulled off her glasses so that Delia could see into her eyes. "I'm always happy to listen, though."

"Okay," she answered numbly. Delia didn't want to talk about it now, but soon.

"Do you want me to get us a flight up to Michigan?"

"I don't know. That will be expensive."

"It will. Nevertheless, I think it's worth the expense, don't you? Is your aunt still living?"

Delia nodded.

"Then we'll go. You should be there for your family, and perhaps you'll see your sister Lilly as well?"

The thought of seeing Lilly again lightened the darkness settling over Delia. "Yes, she will be there of course. Okay, let's go back to Michigan." Delia hugged Alice hard. "Thank you for understanding, Ali."

"No problem. Have a seat and drink some of this lemonade for me please. I'll call the airline right now."

Alice pecked her on the cheek as she walked by.

Delia stopped her and pulled her in for another hug. The smell of her skin was calming. Delia released her and kissed her lightly on the mouth.

Alice smiled her perfect smile, and Delia remembered again why she loved her so much. As one of the beautiful things of the world, Alice's beauty seeped into everything around her.

Delia sat on the wooden lounge chair and sipped Alice's vodka-soaked lemonade. She stared out over the small lake that butted up to their backyard. Only a few cottages dotted the lake. In fact, far more alligators than people populated this area.

Alice said it made her feel primal and adventurous.

Delia told her she was just crazy. She soon learned that the prehistoric reptiles were not the bloodthirsty beasts she'd imagined as a child. The alligators stayed away from their house, and spent most of their time basking in the warm sun and mud along the shores of the lake.

The gators did make swimming in this body of water a no-no, but the beach lay only a few short miles away. So, when the hot summer sun beat too fiercely on their little blue home, they packed a picnic and spent the day on the sand and in the cool ocean surf. The plant life was in full bloom right now, so weeds filled the lake and their yard. Once a week, their neighbor from across the lake came over and mowed their lawn for them. He told them he just loved helping out. Delia believed it was because Alice had 'accidentally' let him catch her sunbathing topless one time and he secretly hoped for a repeat.

I'm going home. The past filled Delia's head. Memories swirled around aimlessly. Don had taken her in and treated her just like another daughter. He had saved her life. Uncle Don had given her many of the skills she used as a nurse. He taught her a deep appreciation of and respect for animal life. The other men at church looked up to him and always stood in line to shake his hand after each service.

He wasn't a talkative man with Delia, but that suited her just fine. She had spent most of her young adult life quietly contemplating her future, and thinking about what her role in society might be. She had been so concerned with where she wanted to go in life that she had neglected the fun things that other young people did.

Still, most of the other young people in her community weren't the orphaned daughters of the local maniac who'd killed his wife and then tried to kill his daughter. Even with all of her baggage, Delia managed to do some normal things. She'd had a boyfriend, Francis, and they'd spent a lot of time together. She'd played with her sister Lilly and completed necessary duties around their house.

Those things seemed normal and right to Delia. But what about now? What was her place now? What would Uncle Don think about her choices? What would her father think about her life? She shook away the thoughts. She wouldn't live out her days just sitting here on the chair by the lake. She would do more, live more, and she knew she would have a partner for all of it. Whatever happened, her choices and their love would lead her.

"All right!" Alice called to her from the house.

Delia got up and walked over to her.

"The first flight available is tomorrow morning."

"Wow, that's soon." Delia said, happy and nervous at the same time. Flying had never been her favorite means of travel, but she shook her discomfort away and gave Alice a warm smile. "Thank you, Ali, that will be just great."

"It is, but it's pretty early, the flight leaves at eight in the morning."

"Oh." They had become accustomed to sleeping late into the morning. "I guess I'm going to have to take you to bed early tonight, won't I?" Delia said with a grin, trying to shrug off her sadness.

"Nope. Tonight, I'm taking you!" Alice gave her a playful smile and took Delia's long-fingered hand. "Are you okay?"

"I am. I've just been away for so long. I meant to go back sooner — it would have been nice to say goodbye."

Alice pulled her close. "Come on, let's get packing. We're going to make a grand entrance back into your home state."

Delia followed Alice into the cozy cottage. They only had one bedroom, but a large sitting area and a spectacular kitchen made up for whatever the home lacked. A huge ceiling fan circulated air around the cottage, keeping the pair comfortable on most days. When night became too hot, they'd sleep naked on top of the covers, letting the breeze from the fan waft over them. That always felt naughty to Delia, like she should at least be a little covered. That naughty feeling often led to a little kissing, and the kissing usually led to something more.

Sex with Alice never failed to amaze her. Their bodies moved as if they'd been made for one another.

Even after five years, their passion still ran deep and true, a hot, fiery, sweaty mess of pleasure.

Alice said their passion was more real and more satisfying because when they made love, they held nothing back. They never said no to a new avenue of satisfaction one of them wanted to explore.

More than just stimulation, more than hot skin and mouths against flesh, their sex was also fun. Alice made her laugh in bed. At first, Delia didn't know how to react to the silliness, but then she let herself go and realized how satisfying a laugh could be, no matter what the situation. They didn't only kiss and touch and feel. They talked to each other about how things felt. They laughed about funny incidents during their days, all while wrapped up inside each other's arms. Delia hadn't had many lovers, only two in fact, but she knew that she and Alice had gotten lucky. She never heard their neighbors scream out in passion like they did. She couldn't imagine happiness any other way.

"Hey," Alice said, and gave her a little shove.

Delia focused again. She had been standing in the hallway, daydreaming. "I want you to take me to bed now, Ali."

Alice grinned. She held her hand out and pulled Delia into their bedroom.

Chapter 16

"What's your aunt going to say when she sees me?" Alice quietly asked Delia as she sat next to her in the taxi during the long, bumpy ride out into farm country.

"I've been wondering that myself," Delia replied. She glanced over at Alice.

Even with her forehead creased with worry, Alice still looked beautiful. Her nervous lips were full and pink.

Delia smiled at her. "Does it matter?"

"Nothing can change how I feel about you. I guess I was just hoping for a heads-up on what I might be walking in to. I don't want to get chased off by a bunch of pitchfork wielding farmers." Alice took her hand and squeezed gently, attempting a smile.

Delia hoped they would be received well by Aunt Deb, but really had no idea. *Lilly will understand, though. She always understood me.* Houses went by in a blur out the window, so many more now than when she'd left... how long ago? More than two years in nursing school, then almost a year overseas, followed by five fabulous years in Florida.

Jesus, eight years since I've been home. Her face twisted up as a pang of guilt coursed through her.

"Hey," Alice shook her a little, "are you okay?"

"I'm a little nervous too. I'm really happy you're going to meet Lilly."

"Me too. I wish that flight had cocktails, though."

Inwardly, Delia sighed. Though she didn't like to talk about it, Alice had developed a drinking habit. Her thoughts drifted back to the dreaded 'dinner of '48' and she quickly shut the memories down. That night, Delia had met Alice's very large, affluent family. On that night, Delia also realized Alice's drinking had become way out of hand.

Delia shuddered at the memory of Alice screaming at her father, "It's my life and I can sleep with women if I want!"

Well, they hadn't seen Alice's family since, just a letter or two from her mother. Now, Delia didn't allow Alice to drink when they left the house. She squeezed her lover's hand. *This will be good for her.*

Michigan looked beautiful. Delia considered fall to be the prettiest of seasons in the north. They passed trees rich with yellow, red, and rust colored leaves. *A good color turn this year.* She remembered some years with hardly a change at all, due to heavy winds and rains that would sometimes blow the leaves from the trees before anyone could enjoy their beauty. She smiled, happy to see the rich splendor once again.

"Did you have a fall color change when you were young?" she asked Alice.

"Are you kidding?" she replied with a wide smile. "I grew up in Grand Rapids, silly, I thought you knew that! We used to play in great big piles of musty leaves every year after we raked them up. Those were some of the best times for my family." Alice paused, remembering. "Before my father was elected to the senate, when things were simpler, the whole family would go out into the yard and we would rake the leaves into a great big pile. Father always let us play in them for most of the afternoon."

Delia's heart warmed seeing the happy memories cross over Alice's face.

"Then when dusk came, father would light the pile and we would have a fantastic bonfire!"

"S'mores?"

"S'mores, of course." Alice trailed off. "Of course we had s'mores." She looked over to Delia. "I love you, Dee."

Delia leaned her head onto Alice's shoulder. "I love you too, Ali."

She looked forward to being home again. She missed her sister, and she missed her aunt. Still, as the car rumbled on past the paved roads, a quiet rushing emerged in her mind. Tiny whispers told her to beware. Something dark drew close.

She pushed her worries aside for the time being. She hadn't been in-tune with her gift in quite some time. During their life in Florida, the two women didn't run into much trouble of the human kind. One or two run-ins with animals had rattled Alice pretty good, and Delia chuckled to herself as she remembered the incident with the 'dragon.'

**

It happened on a warm morning three years ago. While some mornings got just plain hot, this was the perfect kind where Alice could walk out of the house in shorts and a bikini top and be perfectly comfortable. Delia startled in the shower when she heard Alice scream. The sound of her shrill cry chilled Delia to the core, and she leaped out of the shower with the water still running and sprinted through the kitchen, heading for the slider out to the backyard.

"Alice, where are you?" she screamed. As she burst out onto their back patio and into the warm morning sun, she saw Alice standing stock-still at the edge of the yard, staring into the overgrowth beyond the grass. Dense growth lined either side of the lawn and, straight ahead, the pathway to the lake.

"Ali!" Delia yelled as she ran, stricken with panic. "Ali, what happened?"

Alice turned toward Delia and her jaw dropped even further.

"Dee, you're, you're naked!"

Delia looked down. Indeed, she was naked. She'd rushed out of the shower without grabbing a towel and now her exposed body dripped warm water on the grass at her feet. She hadn't cared; protecting Alice her only concern, and getting to her the only thing that mattered.

"What's wrong, Alice? What happened?"

Alice seemed to remember what she freaked out about again because she jumped back from the overgrowth, as if something might come out and get her.

"It's in there! A dragon!"

"What?" Delia huffed, a little frustrated. She strode up to the overgrowth and peered in. Sure enough, a large lizard hid just within the dense cover of weeds and leaves. Not a dragon, of course, but it did have a long body and a protruding snout.

As tall as a small dog, and probably twice as long, the lizard's forked tongue flicked in and out of its mouth. Delia saw movement behind the creature, and imagined a long tail swishing back and forth. She'd seen a picture of this animal before, though she hadn't thought they lived in Florida. For a moment, she felt angry with Alice for frightening her so much, but then her anger gave way and she burst into a fit of giggling.

"What the hell is so funny?" Alice asked, her face flushing red.

"It's not a dragon, honey." Delia laughed harder, and doubled over with the laughter. She fell to the ground, and lay on her side in the cool grass. The dragon apparently had enough of the racket because it turned and quickly disappeared into the jungle of bright green bushes.

"It was huge, Dee. I was scared."

Delia just kept laughing for a moment.

"You know, one of the neighbors across the lake is going to see you like this and then you won't think it's so funny!" Alice had her hands on her hips, looking very stern.

Delia popped up off the ground and jumped into the air, twirling a little as she did.

Alice gaped at her.

"There, I've given them some entertainment," Delia told her with a smirk. "We'll go to the fish and game office today and tell them about the dragon, all right?"

"Really?"

"Really, baby." Delia wrapped her arms around Alice. "I love you, but I'm getting back in the shower. Will you try to stay out of trouble while I'm gone?"

Alice blushed again and nodded.

***

Delia smiled at the memory. They later learned that the dragon was actually an Asian Water Monitor. Their local DNR agent said the monitor was most likely a pet at one time and that the owners had probably released the animal when it grew larger than they expected.

The landscape passing outside her window became more familiar. Far from the city, farm country enveloped them, apparent not from the earth's topography but from what covered it. Where miles of steel and concrete bathed the city, Delia could now see only wheat far out into the horizon. She watched the golden stalks sway lazily in the breeze. Even inside the car, the earthy smell found her and brought back memories she had tucked away years ago.

Then Alice went and said something that ruined it all. She hadn't meant to, of course. No one ever does.

"Do you think Francis still lives around here?" Alice asked.

Delia froze. The corner of her eye twitched a little. Her breath caught deep in her lungs and a cool liquid poured over her heart. Suddenly, the slight whispers that had been quietly rustling through her mind became crystal clear.

She strained to hear words amidst the whispers, but the bumping of the car and the noise of their tires on the gravel road kept her from concentrating. Had the whispers gotten louder as they neared her home town? Delia couldn't tell, but the anxiety she had once felt at the hospital in Liege crept back into her once again.

"Dee? Are you okay, honey?" Alice's voice strained with worry. She had seen the sun drain from Delia's face.

Delia turned to her slowly and nodded. "Yes Ali, I think he's still here."

Alice took her hand and tried to be reassuring. "Don't worry, I'll be here with you."

Delia had a terrible feeling that Alice might not be enough, not if the hatred Francis had felt for her still lingered. She'd put him out of her mind long ago—a selfish thing to do, but she had to move on. Would he try to talk to her if he saw them in Grattan? Would she try to hurt her? Could he still be angry after all these years? The last time she saw him, Francis was confined to a hospital bed, jaw wired shut, eyes burning with hatred.

A wave of guilt rose up but Delia quickly tucked it away. She had come to grips with her actions long ago. She knew now that she never really loved Francis, but she had cared for him deeply and wouldn't have wished his injuries on anyone. She had never intentionally hurt him. What happened between her and Alice was as unavoidable as the sun. Love, real love—a connection brighter and stronger than she'd felt with anyone in her life. She was sometimes so filled with her desire to be with Alice, she thought she might burst.

Delia wanted to come here, needed to come here, but as they crossed the last few miles to her childhood home, she noticed, rather despairingly, that the whispering in her head indeed grew louder. *God, help me get through this visit.* Surely Francis had found out about Don's death, but perhaps he didn't care; maybe he didn't care about her at all anymore. Delia hoped he didn't, but the ominous rushing in her mind clearly disagreed.

No, Francis would find out about Don and he would know that she'd come back. *He'll be waiting.*

She didn't want to think about that, but Delia knew: trouble waited for her in Grattan.

Delia's heart swelled with nostalgia when the old house came into view. Aunt Deb must have heard them approaching, because she waited on the porch, just as she used to when Delia was a child. Delia smiled out the window at her and gave a little wave. *But where is Lilly?* The corners of her smile fell when she realized her sister hadn't come out to greet them. *Perhaps she's in the bathroom or cooking.* Delia chewed the inside of her lip, then Alice's grip tightened on her hand. Delia looked into her eyes for a long moment.

"I love you, Ali."

She nodded. "I love you, too. Can I stay close to you?"

"Definitely."

***

As the late afternoon sun made its way across the sky, a rusty red pickup truck sauntered slowly up the driveway to the butcher's house. Randy McCaul's personal appearance wasn't much better than that of the vehicle he drove. Patchy brown stubble covered his worn leather face, and several teeth had rotted out of his salacious smile, a smile he liked to flash at young girls around town.

The butcher's big, green Chevy 3800 rested in the driveway between the meat barn and the house proper.

As the truck rattled to a stop behind the green pickup, Randy knocked his fist into the center of the steering wheel, causing the horn to bleep briefly before he climbed down out of the truck.

"Jesus," he muttered, drawing in a breath of putrid air from the open window. The stink of decay surrounded the place, a potent mix of aromas somewhere between a honeysuckle bloom and a skunk's ass. Randy had a feeling the butcher had stopped burying the great carcasses of cows out back like his old man had. He probably just piled them up in the woods behind the meat barn. Whatever. He didn't care what the butcher did; he came for his meat order, nothing else. Standing in the dusty dirt driveway, Randy arched backwards and a satisfactory crackle of bones inched up his spine.

The door to the house cracked open and Randy saw the butcher peer out at him, so he offered up a wave.

Then he came out into view. Shirtless, he wore only tattered jeans and dark brown boots covering his body, Randy couldn't help but stare at the butcher, a freak show of shiny, twisted skin. He tried to pry his eyes away as the butcher approached.

He wore a large knife on his hip, strapped to him by the same cracked leather belt that held up his well-worn jeans. As usual, Randy became nervous as the butcher approached.

The man's limp drew more attention to his gross deformities.

Randy had never seen it, but he knew the butcher had a fake leg. The kids around town said it was a human leg that he had cut off someone himself and sewed onto his stump to replace the one he had lost. Silliness, of course. Still, like a frightened dog, the hairs on the back of Randy's neck rose up and he shifted from side to side as he waited.

The butcher came to a stop only a foot away. His grisly form stood several inches taller than Randy, who tried to keep his eyes on the butcher's face and not the mess of scarred flesh across his torso.

The butcher spoke, his voice low and abrupt. "Your meat order is ready."

"Okay, yeah, that's why I came."

The butcher brushed past him toward the meat barn.

"Back your truck up to the overhead door," he said without looking back.

Randy nodded and climbed back into the truck. He never liked being in close proximity to the butcher. Not only did the sight of his mangled body unnerve Randy, the butcher also felt—dangerous. Randy was no coward. He'd fought in the war; he had done his time, thankfully with no injuries. Even so, the butcher made his skin crawl and his heart thump hard in his chest.

"The monster butcher," he mumbled quietly as he started up the old truck. Looking back over his shoulder, Randy backed the truck up to the large gray overhead loading door. Even with the door open, the inside of the barn lay in heavy shadow, and Randy couldn't see the butcher anywhere.

Randy climbed out of the truck once more and made his way up to the barn. The stink of death grew thicker, and Randy cleared his throat against it. He always received good quality meat, he had no worries about that, but he didn't want to spend any more time on this property than necessary. After a minute of waiting by the door, Randy ventured inside.

An area about ten feet deep and twenty feet wide, tacked on to the meat house, this part of the barn had no electricity. Lawn tools—both modern and antique— lay scattered about the ground, including wide variety of cutters, trimmers and edging tools, though from the state of the butcher's property, he didn't invest much time in using these instruments. A large, gas-powered lawn tractor, one of the few he'd ever seen, sat just off to his right. This looked like the one item in the barn that got any real use.

Axes, mauls, two great long band saws, and hatchets lined an entire wall. Several machetes rusted on pegboards and, of course, an ancient scythe. Randy had used all of these instruments growing up on his parents' farm, but looking at them now, thinking of them in the hands of the butcher, sent a chill through his body.

Directly across from him, the door to the meat room stood waiting. The large steel door dripped with condensation and a light fog rolled off its surface before dissipating into the humid air. Randy looked from side to side and, seeing no sign of the butcher, walked up to the door and gripped the handle. Though slick with condensation, the frigid metal turned easily beneath his grip.

A cold blast of air greeted him as he pushed the door open. Skinned carcasses hung from hooks in the ceiling. The thick, metallic stink of blood turned his guts. The door opened just a little farther before a dark form stepped in front of him.

"What are you doing in here?" the butcher asked, looming over Randy. He carried a large box of packed meat: Randy's order.

"I—I was just coming to help you."

The butcher moved toward him without saying a word, forcing Randy to back out of the doorway. He shoved the heavy box of meat into Randy's arms then reached behind him and slammed the door shut. When he turned back to face Randy, his eyes were dark with hate.

"Don't open that door again," he said slowly. "You'll let the cold out."

Randy nodded his head quickly.

"Thanks."

The butcher just stared at him in reply.

"Did you hear your neighbor died?" Randy asked, trying to divert the butcher's attention away from his intrusion.

The butcher only had one eyebrow, but it rose when Randy asked him the question. "What neighbor?"

"I'm surprised you didn't hear. It was Don, the veterinarian just down the road there. Died just two days ago from what I understand."

The butcher's face started doing something Randy didn't quite understand. Twisted flesh twitched and curled, and the corners of the butcher's ruined mouth inched up his face. Though the expression was ghastly, Randy thought he might be trying to smile.

"You can leave now."

"I'll leave now. Thanks." Randy stumbled backward and turned quickly. He tossed the box of meat into his open truck bed and hurried to the driver's door. As he opened the door, he glanced over his shoulder to see the butcher still standing just inside the darkened barn. His arms were crossed over his chest and he glared out at Randy with the same sick smile cut into his face.

Randy raced off the property.

Chapter 17

Alice and Delia walked up to the back porch, each carrying a small suitcase. They held hands. Delia fought hard not to fidget as they approached her Aunt Deb, the woman who had raised her for the second half of her young life.

Deb said nothing as they approached. When Delia stood directly in front of her, she offered a wide smile.

"I missed you so much, Aunt Deb."

Deb eyed her and Alice for a long moment with an expression of curiosity. Delia didn't see anything disapproving in it.

"So, this is what it took to get you to come home, huh?"

Everyone remained quiet for a moment, then Deb stretched her arms out.

"Give your aunt a hug? I could really use one." Deb tried to smile but she just looked sad.

She wrapped strong arms around her aunt. "I'm so sorry, Aunt Deb."

Deb patted her back. "Thank you, Delia. The way that man ate—a half pound of bacon plus sausage and eggs every morning—well, I suppose it was only a matter of time."

At last, they broke their embrace and Delia turned toward Alice.

"Aunt Deb, this is Alice. She's my…she's my girlfriend."

Alice smiled up at her proudly.

"Hello Alice," she said, and extended a hand toward her.

Alice took the hand then stepped closer so she could capture Deb in an embrace of her own. "I'm so sorry for your loss."

Deb nodded appreciatively.

"So," Deb began. "Girlfriends, huh? How does that work? Which one of you does the cooking?"

Delia chuckled and glanced over at Alice again. "Well, that girl can't cook worth a darn."

"And she can't seem to tell the difference between whites and colors in the wash," Alice piped up.

Deb nodded with a small grin. "So you two complement each other well, then."

"We do, Aunt Deb. And more than that, we're happy."

"Well, you'd best come in and have some supper with me," Deb said. Then to Alice, "I'll show you who taught Delia to cook so well."

Delia thought she saw Aunt Deb wink. *Well, this went better than I thought it would.*

***

Delia's Aunt Deb didn't drink, neither had her late Uncle Don, so the house contained no alcohol. Alice lay next to Delia on the tiny twin-sized bed in the upstairs bedroom of her lover's childhood home. Exhaustion and the stress of coming home had worn Delia down and she crashed hard as soon as she hit the sheets.

That left Alice staring up at the ceiling in the not-quite-dark-enough room. Delia snored softly next to her, but she couldn't sleep. She hadn't had a drink all day and she normally had a Bloody Mary or Screwdriver with breakfast, a Rum Runner after lunch, and she would always partake in a little red wine after dinner. Jittery little tremors wriggled through her body.

Alice never felt like she had a drinking problem. She didn't get drunk very often; she just enjoyed having a cocktail now and then. She knew that once in a while she got a little out of hand, but Delia always took care of her. Now, as she stared up at the ceiling, her head buzzed and anxious energy coursed through her body, just enough to keep her awake.

She wanted—no—*needed* a drink. An old blue Dodge sat next to the house. Perhaps she could take that to the store and buy some alcohol. *To the store?* Alice shook her head. She was in the middle of farm country, surrounded by wheat and the sweet stench of cow manure. The closest store, in the heart of the tiny town of Grattan, would have closed down hours ago.

She'd find no city here, no late-night shops for her. She huffed a little more loudly than she'd meant to and Delia's soft snoring paused for just a moment. She tried to keep her eyes pressed closed, but the energy running through her forced them back open again. Why did she come with nothing to drink? It had never occurred to her that there wouldn't be any alcohol in the house. At least gin. *Everyone at least had gin, didn't they?*

Except for this house. Alice pouted silently to herself, but she didn't blame Delia for her discomfort. Delia had to cope with the loss of her uncle and Alice was happy to be here for her. She would go anywhere and do anything for Delia. Next time, she would just have to remember to bring her own medicine. Alice sighed deeply again, and again tensed up as she heard Delia's breathing change. *This is silly.* She couldn't have a drink, but she did have a nearly full pack of cigarettes in her jacket, now flung over the chair in the corner.

Alice slowly rolled herself over the edge of the bed. She dangled one arm and one leg over the side of the shallow bedframe until her fingers felt the cool, dusty surface of the hardwood planks on the floor below. Not polished oak or hickory, like she'd grown up with, but probably an inexpensive pine. She felt the grit that had collected in the porous planks and seams over the years.

With her body supported, Alice carefully swung her other half down onto the floor. Her descent to the floorboards was nearly silent, until her weight lifted off the bed and it creaked with the release. Alice cursed herself, but Delia remained sleeping. She had told Alice to stay with her in the room all night. Delia expressed nervousness about something happening to her, but Delia always overreacted. *I'm tougher than she thinks.* She'd always been able to tackle any problem life threw at her, albeit some with more grace than others.

She did admit that she had begun to lean on Delia for support, but no more so than Delia leaned on her. Alice pulled herself up into a crouch and slowly straightened. She stood slightly hunched to avoid the low ceiling in this child's room. She tiptoed over to the small desk in the corner where her coat hung. She gingerly lifted it off and slipped it over her shoulders.

She wore a silk nightshirt, but preferred to sleep naked from the waist down, so she groped around until she found her flannel lounge pants. Hopping from one foot to the other, she managed to pull on the pants without making too much of a racket. *Jeez, now I'm getting tired.* Sneaking around was exhausting, but a little exciting, too. Alice's lips curled up into a grin at the thought. She had always been one who liked to break the rules, maybe get herself in a bit of trouble now and then. She inched her way across the floor and gently pushed open the wooden door. Thankfully, it opened without a sound. When she slipped out into the hallway, she smiled at herself proudly, like a child who had just gotten away with something. She had made it out of the room without waking her lover.

Alice felt confident in her sneaking abilities as she made her way down a very creaky set of wooden stairs. Her heart thudded loudly in the quiet house. Her lungs burned with anticipation of the sweet relief the nicotine would bring her.

The drafty main floor of the house creeped her out a little. Shadows interlaced across the floor where light from the barn spilled in through the windows in splotches of yellow. Alice felt her way along the walls through the hallway and finally into the kitchen. She peeked out the window over the sink. She could see the barn with its bright sodium light standing sentinel over the yard. Deserted. Of course, it would be at this hour.

Alice slipped out of the kitchen and into the mudroom, then gently eased open the outside door. The old deadbolt complained as she drew it back and she had to caress the door handle firmly to get it to release. At last, she stepped out into the cool night air.

Alice took a deep breath and let it out. Her heart and mind raced. She pulled the pack of cigarettes from her coat pocket and quickly put the thin, paper-wrapped smoke between her lips.

She struck a match, letting it burn for just a moment before touching it to the tip of her cigarette. Then she took a long drag on the smoke, filling her lungs with warm, calming goodness. She instantly felt better and let the first breath out very slowly. As she did, the tension in her body melted away, as if all of her nerves and worries had been exhaled right along with the smoke. She closed her eyes and smiled into the darkness, then raised her hand to take another drag from the cigarette.

A strange sound whirred in the darkness behind her, then something heavy smashed into the back of her head. Alice fell forward off the porch, landing in a tangled heap on the stones below. Her precious cigarette burned on into the night without her.

***

Francis could not believe his luck. After Randy had left with his meat order, he had gone into town to gather information on Don's passing. In a small town like Grattan, everyone knew everything about everyone. *Except me*, Francis thought with a smile. The people thought he looked like a monster, but they had no idea what lurked beneath his puckered skin.

They said a heart attack had claimed the veterinarian's life. *Fools*. Only Francis knew the truth—a dusting of fresh Hemlock in with his morning bacon for a week had done the trick. Sue Squiresby from the ice cream shop thought the funeral had been scheduled for tomorrow, and at the First Presbyterian Church, of course. He had only one question left unanswered, had anyone seen Delia?

No one could say for sure, though one person claimed to have seen her in a taxi coming in from the city. Lilly was away at college in Chicago, and would not return until the next morning, just before the funeral. As far as Francis could figure, with Lilly coming home, Delia would surely be there as well.

So that night, once the sun tucked itself beneath the horizon, Francis set out from his house into the woods on his most important mission. He'd tightly laced up his worn brown boots against his ankles and calves, both the real and the fake. He wore the KA-BAR knife that had been with him through the war strapped securely to his belt. He placed his palm over the end of the hilt, the familiar feel of the forged steel a comfort to him as he trekked along the darkened tree line.

This journey had felt like miles as a child, navigating through the woods to meet up with Delia in the dark of night or after school. Now, he covered the distance quickly. His stump of a thigh ached with each step, but he enjoyed the pain tonight. He was alive again for the first time in years. His face warped into a smile as he picked up speed and loped through the woods, anxious to get to Don's house. He didn't have a plan yet, but he'd always been good at thinking on his feet. On his foot, rather.

Don's house loomed out of the darkness after about thirty minutes. Francis crept up to the edge of the yard and sat down. His leg ached badly now, and he was out of breath. He hadn't done this much hiking since the war, and back then he had two good legs at his disposal. As he sat, rubbing his thigh to dispense the acid burning within, Francis studied the house. Silent and dark, just as he had expected it would be this late at night, with only a single light at the peak of the barn's gambrel roof.

Don's old truck still sat in the gravel driveway up by the barn. No other vehicles sat in the driveway, but she had taken a taxi. *How will I get to her?*

He wondered if she could still be with the harlot who'd stolen her away. *Definitely not.* Even someone as obviously lost as Delia must have realized that such a forbidden and Godless relationship could not continue. *A disgusting abomination.*

His fists clenched as he thought about the woman who had convinced Delia to abandon her life of virtue and her promise to him. She was his, and still would be his if it weren't for that whore. Francis worked to calm his nerves and breathe through the anger he felt. How would he get into the house? After he broke in, he'd have to travel through the whole house to get to Delia's room upstairs. He didn't know how confident he felt in his ability to be silent with his prosthetic leg.

He didn't want to harm Aunt Deb, but if Deb happened to get in the way… He absentmindedly caressed the hilt of his knife again. It called to him, itching for action. A new surety flooded through him. Delia must in the house, just waiting for him.

As well as he could, Francis ran, a crouched-over, hobbling action that took him through the shadows and up next to the barn. He took several deep breaths as he prepared to dash across the driveway bathed in lamp glow from the top of the barn. *My God, they never turn that thing off.* That light had been burning at night since his childhood.

He hesitated when he thought he saw a face in the kitchen window, but looked again and saw nothing. *My Delia is waiting.* Francis ran across the driveway then to the side of the house, where he pressed himself into the shadows at the edge of the back deck. Using only his arms, he hoisted himself up onto the wooden decking. Then he rested. Only for a moment, though, before fate smiled on him for the first time in years.

As he sat in the darkened corner of the porch, the back door gently creaked open and a tall form snuck out. Francis's heart thumped loudly as he watched her. For a moment, he actually worried she might hear it banging in his chest. *Delia?* Could it really be his Delia? He could go to her now and take her away. Take her away so she could be his again. They would live in his house together; they would be a family at last. She would keep her promise to be his wife and to love him forever.

A promise is forever.

Francis felt confident that Delia would see reason and understand why he had gone to such lengths to bring her home. She was obviously lost, lost in the wilderness alone. As her man, he had a duty to guide her back.

With a disciplined slowness that bordered on maddening, Francis raised himself up from the deck. He planted his prosthetic foot firmly so it would not make any noise. The tall woman made her way down the porch steps. Much too tall to be Aunt Deb, this had to be Delia. As she reached the bottom step, bright light from the barn bathed her face. Smooth white skin and deep red hair came into view, and hate boiled over in him. The woman who had taken his Delia stood there.

How dare she come here, to his town? How dare Delia bring her here? The woman lit a cigarette and looked up into the night sky. Francis stood still for a moment, thinking, then he pulled the large KA-BAR knife from its sheaf. He knew what he had to do. With a stealth practiced against long miles behind enemy lines in Europe, he crept up behind the woman. His face hurt from smiling so hard.

Francis positioned himself behind the adulterous whore. He gripped the knife tightly in his hand and swung a huge haymaker at the back of her head. Using the heavy knife handle as a bludgeon, he slammed it into the back of her skull. His fist connected with her head with a loud *thunk*! She dropped to the ground at the same time his hand exploded in pain. *Shit!*

He'd broken his hand against her skull. For the moment, he could still uncurl his fingers, so he shoved the heavy KA-BAR into its sheath once more. Francis looked down at his prize. *This is how I will get my Delia to come to me.* As a plan formed in his mind, it twisted and became more dangerous with every second. He stepped down off the porch and bent over to haul the woman up off the ground. Then he had another thought and pulled his knife back out.

Turning back to the wooden deck, he knelt down and began carving into the porous surface with the tip of his knife. After five minutes of scraping, Francis's hand pulsed with bright hot pain. He had to get moving before the adrenaline let up. Sliding the knife back into its sheath once again, gingerly this time as he could barely move his hand, he headed back down the steps to his unconscious prey.

Francis bent down and put an arm around her chest beneath her arms. Then he heaved up with all of his strength and flung her over his shoulder. His muscles screamed like babies but he shushed them quickly. He shuffled the woman around until she laid out behind his head and over both shoulders. *Just like doing a squat press in basic training*, he thought.

The first step proved the hardest. As all of his weight and the woman he carried came down on the prosthetic, a shot of hot pain burned into his stump. He felt the skin tearing under the added weight. Still, he held the position, letting his body absorb the pain and acclimate to it. It didn't take long for a cool numbness to replace the white-hot heat. He nodded to himself and started his journey back through the woods. He looked behind him as he took the last steps out of Don's yard. The house stood in silence, unknowing or uncaring about what had just transpired.

As he trampled slowly through the woods, he began humming to himself contentedly. His mother's voice played in his head.

Come tip toe through the window
By the window is where I will be
Tip toe through the tulips with me

Mother had been gone many years now. He missed her, and he wondered what life would have been like had she not died. Now he had a purpose, though, and she'd be proud of him. Carrying the woman like a sack on his shoulders, he felt good for the first time in a long time. As he walked toward home, the prosthetic ground deeper into his stump. Blood and bits of torn skin leached out and dribbled down the wooden leg. He focused on the task in front of him, his plan to get Delia back. He would make her see that they belonged together.

Black trees moved past as he hummed his way through the woods. His mood was light even with the heavy load he carried. His brain buzzed with many thoughts, but only one dominated: Delia. When Delia left him, his life went to shit. If she'd stayed faithful to him, he never would have lost focus in the war, and he never would have been injured. Moreover, he wouldn't have a deep pit where his heart should be. With Delia back, he would feel something other than pain and regret. The balance of his life would be restored and all the wrongs would be righted. He may actually be happy.

Chapter 18

"Wake up!" A loud whisper screeched angrily in her ear, startling Delia from sleep.

The sun had not yet dawned when Delia woke, confused and alone. No sooner had she opened her eyes than a deafening roar of angry voices assaulted her.

Her arms flew out to the side, reaching for Alice. Nothing. Delia sat bolt upright in her tiny bed.

Under normal circumstances, she'd have assumed Alice woke up early and went outside to smoke or indulge in her morning Bloody Mary. The raucous noise in her head told her something very different had happened. The voices built up a dizzying pressure within her.

"Ahh!" she cried out, pressing her hands to the sides of her skull. *Where the hell is Ali?* It felt like the hospital all over again. Her thoughts drifted back to the morning Francis attacked Alice in Belgium.

Delia forced herself to stay still for a moment. Her stomach rolled with anxious nausea. *Be still, just be still.* Her lips trembled and her hands shook, but she concentrated her thoughts and focused her mind, forcing down the waves of noise so she could think for a moment.

He's taken her. He's taken my Alice.

She needed to dress first and she did so quickly, leaving her nightshirt on and slipping her legs into the pair of pleated slacks she had worn the previous day. Aunt Deb would still be in bed, but Delia would not burden her with the knowledge of what must have happened during the night. She stopped only to use the bathroom before heading out through the kitchen to put on her shoes, then on to the back porch. None of it felt real to her yet, like a terrible waking dream.

How could he have taken her? When she reached the back door, she saw that it was unlocked but the window was intact. Nothing indicated that the door had been forced open.

Delia stepped out like the walking dead, forcing her feet forward into the dim morning. She saw the carving on the ancient deck boards immediately. Delia staggered forward and dropped down to her knees next to the scarred wood. Even in the low light of pre-dawn, she couldn't miss the crude artwork. Tears welled up in her eyes and suddenly the mental hold she had against the horrible roaring in her head broke free and the sound crashed through her again.

The overwhelming force of emotions caused her to swoon, and she fell against the porch, landing with her cheek against the letters carved there. As her consciousness waned and her head swam, lost in a lifetime of confusing memories and feelings, she found herself remembering the day she had first seen those letters carved into wood.

***

"So everyone knows we're together," Francis said as he worked his knife into the smooth bark of the large beech tree that Delia leaned against.

She observed him curiously. He had carved a large heart into the skin of the tree, which he was now filling with letters. "We're in the middle of the forest, I don't think this will be a good place for an advertisement," she said.

Francis paused and looked over at her. As usual, his dark brown hair was a disheveled mess, falling over his eyes so that he had to brush it away to see her. As he stared at her, he smiled. His face was terribly handsome. His eyes, a warm chocolate, filled with what he called love as he looked at her.

Delia repeated those words back to him, the 'I love you' words, but she didn't really know what they meant.

She felt desire and attraction as she admired his finely shaped body and his rough face. But that was lust. *Maybe Francis thinks they're the same thing.* Having accidentally discovered the art of masturbation one evening after a bath, she knew what lust felt like, and had indulged herself on every bath night since then. But love was something different entirely.

She never told Francis about the bathroom sessions. They were only sixteen, and while the sweet confusion of pubescent hormones had begun coursing through both of them, they were still largely innocent. Sure, there had been kissing over the years, mostly initiated by Francis, and while she enjoyed the kissing, as well as his hands when they roughly groped over her breasts, she just didn't feel as passionately about it as he did. None of it seemed to compare to the time she had spent alone in the bathroom. She kept trying, though, so now, as he stared into her eyes, she gave him a warm smile.

"But I do think it's lovely, Francis."

Francis gave up a large crooked grin and turned back to his work. "We know it's here, Dee, and we're the only ones that matter, aren't we?"

Delia hesitated. She knew what Francis would like to hear, but in her heart, completing school with perfect grades so she could enter a good vocational school and become successful mattered more than anything else. Other things also mattered much more than the two of them: bankers, mortgages, jobs, houses, children. But Delia didn't say any of those things. Instead, she replied only, "Yes, of course."

Delia stared off into the woods around them. The musky smell of earth enveloped everything. Her hair looked pretty today, blonde curls that bounced lightly above her shoulders. He had been toying with the buoyant curls enough that she'd had to slap him away, lest he pull apart her hard work.

"I need to return home, soon," she told him.

"I'm almost done here, Dee."

"All right, then."

"There!" Francis exclaimed triumphantly. He stepped away from the old tree and held his hand out to her. Then he pulled her next to him to observe his artistry. Carved into the flesh of the tree was *Francis + Delia* surrounded by a slightly misshaped heart. Delia sighed to herself and patted his hard chest with her palm. He sweated profusely, even with his shirt sleeves rolled up to his elbows, revealing his heavily muscled forearms.

Delia leaned over and kissed him deeply on the lips, she knew he really enjoyed it when she did. She wrapped one hand behind his neck and squeezed a little, putting more pressure into their kiss, then pulled away abruptly.

"You did a nice job. All of the forest creatures will know not to mess with me." Delia gave him a playful look then drew him away from the tree. "I need to return home now. Walk me there?"

"Of course," he replied. They started to walk, but Francis stopped suddenly and pulled her close. He stared intently into her eyes, a dark and troubled cloud over his face. "You know we're meant to be together, don't you?"

His voice sounded too serious and his broad chest suddenly seemed intimidating. The tendons in his neck stood out and his breaths came out hard. Delia felt an irrational shiver of fear. She didn't hesitate in responding, not even for a moment. "Of course I know that, Francis. I love you. Now please walk me home."

His face softened at her response. "Of course, I'm sorry. Sometimes I just worry about you."

"Well you needn't worry about me, Francis. Now hustle up, I'm nearly late for dinner."

As Delia pulled Francis along, her mind filled with an odd sound, like a hard wind blowing around them, but the trees weren't moving. She had heard that sound before, and as they walked, she started to recollect where. Ever since her mother died, Delia had felt something *else* in her head. She didn't talk about or think about the unshaped thing within her.

The sound died down into a gentle rustling, but Delia couldn't shake the strange feeling of unease. For the first time in a long time, she felt fearful. She couldn't do anything about it, though. Their paths were locked together in the dance of time now, more so than she would have ever imagined.

***

Delia startled back into consciousness to find herself collapsed on the deck in the early morning sunlight. The dream faded and the roar of worried thoughts pounded against her skull once more. She lifted herself from the deck, noticing a large and unfortunate lump where her forehead had connected with the wood. She traced her fingers over the carved heart in the old boards. Inside the heart were the same words he'd carved into the tree so many years ago: *Francis + Delia.*

He still thinks I belong to him. Back then, he felt like the carving in the tree was his pledge to the world that they belonged to each other. In his mind, that pledge and that agreement would last forever. Then another, more worrisome thought popped into her head. If he had time to carve all of this, he must have hurt Alice. Yes, he would have incapacitated her somehow. He had no doubt taken her to draw Delia to him. She only hoped he hadn't killed her yet, because she knew that had to be his end game. Though she hadn't seen or heard from Francis in years, it appeared that, in his mind, Alice was all that stood between them.

She had to take the bait. She had no choice but to go after Alice. Not only her friend and lover, Delia felt like Alice was a part of her very core, of her existence. No one person could be flawless, but together, she and Delia made something more than perfect. Delia thought of Alice as her wife, but the more accurate word was soulmate.

Delia finally gathered her senses, stood up and looked off toward Francis's house. Crisp white light streamed out over the yard, causing tiny diamonds of dew to sparkle on the grass. The underbrush beyond glittered with wet, reflective jewels as well. She had spent many mornings on this very porch with her sister Lilly, watching the sun come up, always in awe of nature's sparkling light show. It had seemed like their own private miracle.

Today held none of that magic. Delia stepped down from the porch and headed straight through the yard into the thick tree line that ran parallel to the great wheat fields beyond the farm. Delia didn't look back at the farm as she left. She knew she might not return, but she had to try, for Alice's sake and for her own. She hoped she wasn't heading toward her own funeral. She should have called the sheriff, should have woken Aunt Deb, but all she could think about was getting to Alice.

The woods were unforgiving on her inappropriate clothing. Her slacks caught on every bramble she attempted to step over and soon, bracelets of burrs adorned her ankles. Sharp branches poked and tore her thin cotton nightshirt. She hacked away with her bare hands and arms, frustrated with the slow progress. Then she began to run. Trees whipped and cut and scraped her, and she pushed harder

It had been years since she had actually run, and the flats she wore were not designed for running through bushes and trees. Several minutes went by before her legs found a hard rhythm. She ran hard, and her feet glided through the underbrush.

Her shoulders bobbed through the branches instinctively as her body found the rhythm of its childhood once more. Her breath came hard, but the burn within her lungs was a welcome distraction from the terror and worry she felt.

The noise in her mind had become so great that the waves of sound careening through her head actually appeared to take shape. Shadows darted through her vision. They twisted and moved, dancing in front of her.

Maybe this is a visual migraine? She'd heard about the strange phenomenon from a Belgian doctor, but this felt more connected with the whispers in her mind. It appeared her special gift had evolved further.

Just what I need.

The shapes didn't impede her vision; they were simply a part of it. As she ran through the white morning light, the strange shadows branched out and tread alongside her. Her eyes darted back and forth through the woods as she observed the shadowy forms. They looked more and more human, crouching down beside trees, examining the ground before darting forward once more.

What the hell is happening here?

Confusion swam into her already overcrowded mind and she forced it away. She couldn't think about this strange phenomenon now, couldn't think about how crazy she had become.

It's all in my head anyway.

She needed to focus on moving through the woods quickly. The dissonant roar had quieted some, or perhaps the sound of her own heavy breathing masked it. Either way she plodded on, harder and faster with each stride.

Her legs held fast and strong, and she covered the distance quickly. In only fifteen minutes, the butcher's house loomed beyond the trees. Instead of heading straight to the house and into Francis's ambush, Delia opted to be a little sneakier and a lot more careful.

She changed directions and skirted around the yard, still hidden in the trees, until she came up behind the meat house. Long ago, Francis had shown her the secret back door to the meat house, where his father would come to smoke his special tobacco. Delia's gait slowed to a walk. The pungent smell of rotting meat hit her hard, and when she broke through the edge of the tree line behind the barn, she saw why.

Through a black cloud of flies, a heaping pile of mutilated cow and pig carcasses appeared. *Jesus Christ, he isn't even burying them; he's just throwing them behind the barn.* Delia choked down the bile gurgling up in her throat and leaped the last few feet up to the back door. She nervously placed a hand on the knob. *What if it's locked?* She turned the handle. The door swung open into the cold darkness of the meat room.

Chapter 19

Alice woke with a blinding headache, in an unfamiliar place. She remembered sneaking downstairs to have a cigarette, but nothing beyond that. Now she lay on a patch of dry earth, with rocky soil digging into her ribs. As she tried to lift herself from the ground, panic set in. She'd been bound, hand and foot, her wrists tied together behind her back.

"Help!" she cried out. "Somebody help me! Delia!"

"Don't you worry," a deep, rusty voice said from behind her. "I'm sure she'll be here soon."

Alice flopped like a fish until she lay flat on her back and face to face with the man. She gasped when she saw him. *He's a monster.*

Even after years of work as a nurse in the army corps, dealing with everything from burns to bullet holes and amputations, she could not deny that this man was truly hideous. His disfigurement went deeper than his scarred skin. Something evil filled his eyes.

She didn't yet realize his identity.

"You, you kidnapped me?" she asked in a frightened voice. "Why did you do that? What do you want from me?"

"I don't want anything from you, whore. I want what's mine. I want my Delia back."

Shock smacked her in the face. "Francis," she breathed.

The man nodded. "It was foolish for you two to come back here. She belongs to me, you know. She promised to be mine forever."

Alice shook her head frantically.

"A promise you made her break!" he yelled.

"No, I didn't," Alice pleaded. "We fell in love!"

Francis hissed at her. "She was mine and you took her from me. Now I'll take her back."

"She doesn't belong to you or me. Delia made her choice, and she chose to be with me." Francis stood and planted his prosthetic firmly on the ground then swung his other foot at her, smashing it into the side of her skull.

As the world went black around Alice, she heard him say. "She *is* mine."

***

Alice's head felt like an explosion went off inside it. She regained consciousness and immediately wished she hadn't. The intense, throbbing pressure felt like it might outright kill her. After two severe traumas to the head in one day, Alice knew she must be concussed. The sticky dryness in her mouth indicated dehydration as well.

"Well, I think I'm about ready for you."

Alice startled, then did her fish flopping maneuver once more so she could see Francis. He stood a few paces away over a gaping hole in the earth, with his shirt off and a shovel in his hand. She didn't know his intensions yet, but panic surged through her nonetheless.

"Ah yes, you have every right to be scared," he continued, seeing the fear in her eyes, "because this will be the end of the road for you." Francis graced her with one of his hideous smiles.

"Help! Help me!" Alice screamed. Francis's laughter punctuated her cries.

"That's it, girl, just keep at it!" He continued to laugh as he walked up to her, leaving the shovel by the hole he'd dug.

Alice tried to flop away from him, which elicited another chuckle from Francis.

He stooped down and grabbed her by the arms.

"Come admire my hard work, why don't you?" With that, he dragged her over to the deep hole he had torn into the yard.

Alice tried to wriggle out of his grip, but with her hands and feet bound, she stood no chance against the large man.

Francis pulled her right up to the edge of the pit so she could look down into it.

"You may want to stand on your tippy toes, I'm not sure I got the depth just right," he snarled at her, then shoved her feet first into the hole.

Alice screamed as she fell and landed in a crumpled pile atop her bound ankles. A moment later, she felt a pile of dirt smack the top of her head.

"It might be a little quicker that way, but I'd stand up if I were you."

Alice wriggled herself against the sides of the narrow hole to get into a standing position. Only a couple of body widths in diameter, and five and a half feet deep, the pit resembled a cylinder cut straight into the ground. Black dirt rained down on her from above. She did indeed need to stand on her tippy toes, and when she got herself upright, just her head protruded above the earth.

He's burying me alive.

Terror chewed away her nerves like a hungry beast. Anytime she tried to move out of the position he wanted her in, Francis whacked her in the face with the shovel. It seemed to take him hours to fill her grave. When the dirt reached her breasts, the weight of it pressed against her chest. Her panicked lungs heaved, demanding more room. It felt like suffocating.

Alice began to cry, and Francis started singing. The song, soft and melodious, sounded disturbingly happy coming from a heinous monster.

"And if I kiss you in the garden

In the moonlight

Will you pardon me?

Come tip toe through the tulips with me"

Alice's voice gave out on her, so she simply watched, wheezing helplessly as Francis worked to complete her tomb. *I'm going to die. Please don't come, Delia. Don't let him get you too.* Even as she thought it, she knew she didn't mean it. She didn't want Francis to get to Delia, but she did want to be saved. Her life couldn't be over, not this young, and not this way.

Though it dwindled quickly, she still held a small amount of hope. Delia had told her she would always look after her, and Alice believed her. *Please save me, Dee.*

The weight of her tomb went from uncomfortable to excruciating. As Francis piled more dirt around her, the earth's embrace became heavier, and her lungs struggled to inflate. Her body fought to suck in air, but the harder she fought, the less air she drew. More tears fell down her face.

She'd been strong and resilient her whole life, but not today. Perhaps she had let herself go, perhaps the practiced strength she had learned from years of boarding school teachers had begun to wane. She'd survived and overcome great obstacles, but now she wept like a baby. It wasn't Francis torturing her now but her own weak emotions. She had lived well for a long time. *Is it just my time to go?* No, it couldn't be.

The nurse that had been tucked away within her for years explained to Alice, as calmly as she could, that her lungs weren't working properly. Because of their reduced function, her blood and therefore her brain couldn't receive the oxygen they needed. Her thoughts felt airy and scattered, but muddled with pain and filled with weepy emotion. *I have to slow my breathing. If I can't slow my breathing, I'm going to black out.*

Easier said than done. Alice tried to listen to the small sane voice inside her. She focused on taking slow, shallow breaths, retraining her lungs to accept the shortened breaths. She almost had it under control, almost, until he spoke again. Buried up to the neck, she could no longer turn her head, so Francis came and lowered himself down into an awkward squat in front of her. He stank with sharp, thick body odor. Beaded sweat ran off him in strange patterns following the twisted scar tissue that covered half of his body.

"You're all set here," Francis said lightly. He sounded happy, excited. Francis looked around the yard. "She's nearby, I think. I can feel her."

"What are you going to do to her?" Alice asked, her voice no more than a whisper.

Francis cocked his head at Alice curiously. "What am I going to do to her?" His eyes turned angry, and his hand shot out and caught a handful of her hair. He gripped it tightly and pulled her head back.

"Once you're gone, I'm going to love her! I'm going to marry her! We'll have a proper family, not this charade of a life you tricked her into!"

"I never tricked her into anything," Alice cried in a soft voice.

"Once you're gone, I'll make her happy." With that, Francis stood. "I expect her soon, so I need to get ready. You should make yourself ready, too."

With that, Francis stood and walked away, continuing his strange song.

"Tip toe from your pillow
To the shadow of a willow tree
And tip toe through the tulips with me
Just me dear
In flowers we'll stray
And we'll keep the April showers away"

Alice watched as he walked out of her line of sight. She choked on her tears, barely able to breathe enough to cry properly. Though she fought it, blackness threatened to consume her, both mentally and physically. *Help me, Dee. Help me.*

***

Cold and rotten, the air in the meat room sank into Delia's bones. As the steel door closed behind her, gooseflesh rose over her sweaty body. From metal hooks all around her hung the butchered bodies of cows and pigs. Delia thought she saw a horse hanging in the center of the room. *Who would eat a horse?* Many people would, she supposed, if they got hungry enough.

Just the thought of the meat room disturbed her, and now being in it, her skin crawled. Each step she took brought her into contact with another piece of cold, dead meat, but she had no choice but to keep moving forward. She had to put soft, feminine Delia aside and remember the tough farm girl she had once been. She could get through this maze of death. *It's only meat, after all.* As a girl she had been very aware of where all of their food came from.

Years of eating in restaurants and shopping in grocery stores for neatly packaged dinners made it easy to forget where they got that food. When she ate meat, an animal had to die. *This is all just food.* She tried to look at the hanging hulks with more detachment, watching them sway slightly as she passed by. A yellow light glowed at the far end of the long room. Other than that, only cold darkness reigned.

Even so, her eyes adjusted enough to pick out the grisly details around her. Halfway through the room, she stumbled over her own feet and went off course, crashing into a cold slab of meat. She put her arms out and used the nearly frozen meat to pull herself back to her feet. Delia recovered quickly, until she realized the large mass of cold flesh wore clothes.

"Oh my God," she whispered, recoiling quickly.

She stood stock-still, waiting as her startled eyes adjusted and a face emerged from the blackness. Whitish-blue from cold and blood loss, with skin sagging off the bones, Francis's older brother Larry stared at her with empty eyes. Her hand flew up to her mouth and she screamed in the darkness.

Larry hung from a great steel hook in the ceiling, just like the other animals. On trembling legs, Delia walked back up to Larry's body. He wore a white cotton shirt, just like he always had. His pants were missing, though. A deep red opening on the underside of his belly drew her attention. She lifted his shirt, then retched. His belly, which had been large in life, was wrinkled and deflated like a popped balloon. The gaping wound to his lower abdomen told the story. Francis had opened his belly and let his entrails fall out. *Gutted like an animal.*

Tears prickled at the corners of her eyes. Delia didn't cry for Larry, a vile man who reveled in the torture of his younger brother, a true bastard. She cried for Francis, and she cried for Alice. Had she helped to create this monster? The shivering cold penetrated far deeper than her skin and Delia thought she may never warm from it. She knew Francis had been dangerously obsessed with her as a young man. She should have known he would snap when she left him. In the arms of her new lover, it had been all too easy to ignore the consequences.

Now she lived those consequences. A deranged killer had her soul mate. *I have to save her.* But how? How could she hope to win? Francis, strong and calculating, had the advantage on his own turf.

Delia's resolve cracked. Seeing Larry's body tipped her over the edge of an invisible precipice and she now dangled by only threads. She closed her eyes and forced several deep breaths into her lungs. When she opened them again, she wasn't alone.

The shadowy figures who had run with her in the woods, the ones she had somehow manifested, had joined her in the cooler. Amongst the slabs of hanging beef, horses, and Larry, the translucent specters stood. They waited, but for what she didn't know.

"What are you?" she called out quietly. Her breaths left clouds of white fog in the frigid room. The smoky shapes shifted, but offered no answer.

I have completely lost my mind. I'm speaking to my imagination.

"Are you the voices I hear? What do you want? What should I do?"

The shadow closest to Delia stretched out a flat, gray appendage. While it had no defining features, she knew the creature offered her its hand. Surprising herself, Delia reached out toward it. Instead of letting her touch it, the figure moved away. Then with its silken appendage, the creature beckoned for her to follow. As her feet began to move, so did the rest of the apparitions, following behind and around her as she traversed the rest of the macabre room.

She didn't understand her strange guides, but they gave her comfort. When she reached the end of the meat locker and cracked the door open, blinding sunlight streamed in. Delia put a hand up over her eyes and inched out the rest of the way. Before closing the door behind her, she ventured a last look inside.

A table stood close to the door, with a variety of tools laid haphazardly across it, including a long, metal-handled filet knife. Delia reached over and plucked the knife from the table, gripping it tightly in her fist. The metal warmed quickly in her hand. *Ok, I'm ready now.*

Delia stepped out from under the overhang of the barn, and through the opened overhead door. From this vantage point she could see most of the yard and the house directly in front of her. No Francis, and no Alice. They had to be either inside or behind the house, near the trail that led to the small fishing pond where Francis had taken her as a child. She remembered that day very clearly.

"That was the day Buster died," she murmured, remembering with terrible clarity how Larry had killed Francis's dog.

No sooner had the recollection of Buster's death emerged in her mind than she heard the riding lawnmower start up.

"Oh my God." He had no use for a hostage, Francis only wanted Delia back. Why else would he bring Alice to this place? Delia's stomach lurched.

He's going to kill my Ali.

Delia's feet moved automatically and she sprinted toward the house, knowing that Francis would be around the back.

"Alice!" she screamed as loud as she could. "I'm here Alice!" Her arms pumped hard as she ran, the shining steel of the knife flashing dangerously close to her in the sunlight.

"Hang on baby, I'm coming!"

Chapter 20

Francis's leg ached fiercely. His swollen stump burned, the skin scraped raw from too many hours on the prosthetic. When this day was over, he would have Delia draw him a bath with Epsom salts. The salts soothed his muscles and kept infection away. He smiled at the thought of Delia working around the house for him.

He made his way over to the small outbuilding where he had left the riding mower. Though a hardy machine, the mower had rusted badly, and the metal struts that held the cutting apparatus in place had barely hung on through the ravages of time. With brutally cold winters and summers drenched in humidity, things just didn't last in Michigan. He rattled the frame of the machine once; noting that one strut in particular had nearly come free.

"Can't have any hiccups during the big show," he said to himself, and set about finding a crescent wrench. He located the correct tool, but when he tried to pick it up, the wrench fell right out of his hand.

"What the devil?" he muttered, looking down at his right hand. Dark maroon and severely swollen, the hand looked like a roast that had been left out too long.

"Shit." He'd been so focused on the task of digging the hole and burying Alice that he had blocked out the increasing pain in his hand. Now the nerves lit up as if on fire, sending acidy tendrils through his arm. *Goddamn woman broke my hand.*

Of course she had. It had been a foolish but necessary thing to do. The small bones of the hand weren't made to withstand a hard impact into a person's skull, a bone that *was* designed to withstand impacts. Using a long-practiced pain managing meditation, Francis willed the gnarled fingers to curl. He nodded as they slowly responded.

"Guess I'm a lefty today." He scooped up the wrench with the two fingers of his still-functioning hand and went about tightening a bolt on the frame of the old rider. Satisfied, he flopped down onto the ground and manually turned the blades, running a finger along their surface to ensure sharpness of the edges. He had hand-filed the twisting metal blades only a few months ago, a painstaking task that had consumed most of an afternoon.

"This will do the job," he muttered to himself. "Just need to gas her up."

The old red gas can waited nearby and he emptied its contents into the beastly machine. Tossing the can aside, Francis climbed atop the mower and started the engine. Like a good omen, the little combustion engine roared to life on the first try. The vibration shivered through the machine and made his bones hum. He smiled. *Excellent.* Delia should be making her way to his house now, he figured, and he would have a surprise for her when she arrived.

"I'm going to set you free, my love. Free to love me the way you should." He put the mower in gear and the blades spun. He beamed, and as his feet worked the pedals, Francis made a beeline to where he'd buried Alice behind his house. The time of reckoning had come, and he would be the instrument of justice exacted upon her.

***

Alice tried to wriggle her way free as soon as Francis walked away.

It didn't have the effect she expected. The crumbled earth around her settled even further as she struggled, the slightly damp clay and black earth compacting, resulting in even more pressure against her body. Her feet lost feeling first, and thank God for that, because for a while they were burning, as if being stabbed by needles and having hot water poured on them at the same time.

The pressure against her chest crushed out every breath she managed to take in. Her feeble attempts to escape had left her buried even tighter, each breath a shallow and painful pant—not enough to keep her mind functioning correctly. She kept blacking out, the world spinning into a fuzzy gray haze then disappearing completely.

As Alice drifted in and out of consciousness, sometimes she came back to the farm and sometimes back home to Florida. She lay in bed with Delia, tracing her fingers across her bare skin, watching the tiny hairs along her body rise to meet her touch. Delia would roll over and look at her, her cool blue eyes still full of sleep. They would kiss and Delia's hands would lovingly caress her body, which begged for her touch. She would tell her how much she loved her.

"I love you too," Alice whispered.

Then Delia screamed.

"Dee? What's the matter, baby?" Alice mumbled, confused.

"I'm here Alice!" Delia screamed.

Alice didn't understand. "You're already here, Dee."

"Hang on baby, I'm coming!"

Delia kissed her softly on the lips, and started to disappear. Then the bedroom disappeared, and with it went Florida.

"No, no, come back! I don't want to be alone." Her vision went out. When it came back, Alice could see only grass and dirt in front of her. The smell of earth and the reeking stench of decay filled her nostrils.

In the distance, she thought she could see movement, but she couldn't focus. Then a grinding roar filled the air and the ground hummed. The dirt around her chest shook and compressed further. Too soon, her vision cleared and she saw the monstrous riding mower thirty yards in front of her.

Francis sat atop the beast, his eyes trained on her, his face twisted up in that awful smile he had. Alice's eyes locked onto the spinning contraption of blades headed straight for her head. The mower didn't move fast, but it didn't have much distance to cover. She estimated only thirty seconds before he reached her. *Goodbye Dee.*

Alice lived beyond panic, in a barely conscious state of tangible fear. The world slipped in and out and away from her. *Maybe that's best*, she thought, *maybe that means it will hurt less.* She hoped. The last of her will and emotions leaked out onto the ground as salty tears. Then she saw another movement. She blinked several times to clear the tears from her eyes.

At first it only looked like a shadow, but the lines solidified, and Alice saw a figure streaking through the yard from around the side of the house. *Oh my God, it's my Delia!* She ran faster than humanly possible, flowing across the yard like her feet hovered above the ground.

Even at a distance, she could see the fire of determination burning in Delia's eyes. She gained ground on Francis impossibly fast. She would catch him, Alice felt sure of it, but what then? Francis could do away with her easily, couldn't he?

No, Delia will save me.

Delia soared through the air toward the growling mechanical beast.

***

Delia's feet skimmed over the top of the mangy grass so quickly that it seemed like she raced through air itself. It didn't take long to reach the house, and less as she sprinted around the side of it. The shadowy creatures kept pace beside her. As she ran, they congealed into one large, gray mass that enveloped her. *This just keeps getting stranger.*

Then the house disappeared, and Delia flew over the ground behind the butcher's battered old home. The mower stood only ten yards in front of her and to the right. He must have come from around the other side of the house. Her frantic eyes found Alice a moment later. *Jesus!*

Her love, her life—buried up to her neck only twenty-five yards away—wept. Delia despaired, she couldn't get to Alice before the mower did.

But I don't have to reach her, she thought, her grip tightening on the knife, *just the mower.* She sprinted directly for Francis.

The blades on the front of the great beast left the rear unprotected. He sat atop the machine, his face hard and his eyes locked on Alice. He never saw Delia coming. With an engine built for power not speed, she caught up quickly.

Delia had no plan for what she needed to do when she reached the mower, only that she had to stop it. She came within five feet of the mower only a few yards from Alice's head.

It's now or never.

She leapt from the ground, summoning every ounce, every grain of strength she possessed and flew through the air. For one terrifying moment she thought she'd jumped too soon, because it looked like she would miss the back of the tractor altogether. But the wind carried her long body, and Delia landed painfully on her knees right behind Francis.

The jerking of the mower nearly threw her off backwards, and her arms wind-milled to keep her steady. To her utter dismay, she lost her grip on the knife and it tumbled out of her hand. Her only weapon hit the side of the tractor then bounced off over Francis and onto the ground. *Now what do I do?*

Alice had only seconds left to live, and Delia had no weapon to use against a trained killer.

Chapter 21

He should have been watching his surroundings better. One of the vital rules in all combat situations was to maintain a 360 degree view of the situation. But Francis felt comfortable on his property, and this wasn't combat, but resolution to a problem, fixing a wrong that had gone unaddressed for years. Still, he should have been paying more attention, for if he had, things may have ended differently. But with the target of his rage only a few short yards away, he focused solely on that. He'd seen no sign of Delia coming out of the tree line from the direction of her childhood home. While he didn't want her to miss the show, his vengeance could wait no longer.

Adjusting a long handle on his left, Francis lowered the cutting blades to just a few inches off the ground. *It's going to be messy*, he thought, then, *I need to replace this mower anyway*. He never heard Delia coming over the clatter of the engine, but he felt the thump behind him and the mower's weight shift when she landed on the back of it. A glint of metal flipped through his vision and clattered over the mower in front of him.

Huh?

Startled, Francis quickly turned to look over his left shoulder.

Delia stared him dead in the eyes as she lunged toward him.

For a moment, he thought she was leaning over to kiss him, and Francis smiled. It didn't last long.

With a tug at his belt, Delia wrestled his KA-BAR from its sheath.

What the-

Francis didn't have time to finish the thought. With two hands, Delia raised the stolen knife over her head. He tried to dodge to the right but she brought the blade down with surprising speed. The great knife sunk straight down into the top of his left shoulder. He screamed as fierce pain lanced through him and he slumped forward, releasing the pressure on the accelerator. *Dammit!*

His arm went numb. *Dammit, woman!* The mower lurched to a stop, throwing Delia forward on top of Francis. As she fell into his lap, Francis's strong hands immediately clamped down on her shoulders.

His task wasn't done, but it felt good having Delia this close to him again. The engine rattled in an uneasy idle. His eyes softened as he gazed at Delia. He would forgive her for attacking him. He had to. She was his true love. *It isn't her fault.* Until the other woman was dead, Delia would still feel like she had to obey her. Still, Delia stared at him with such longing in her eyes. He let his hands soften against her. He rubbed them over the sleeves of her white nightshirt, feeling the warm skin beneath. Her shirt had a low, oval neckline and he could just see the curve of her breasts beneath. A strange tingling enveloped the left side of his body. Despite the injury, he felt himself aroused as he let his mangled right hand play across the front of Delia's shirt. She pressed her chest forward a little and suddenly Francis felt a nipple beneath his fingers. His mind clouded over. *My Delia has come back to me.* At last.

She would probably even help him dispose of the other woman, now that she realized where she belonged. She leaned in close and pressed her lips against his. He felt like he would explode, then Delia's tongue found his lips and she forced it into his mouth. The sweet sensation overwhelmed him, and Francis let his head fall back in ecstasy.

His shoulder exploded in pain.

He felt as if a giant tore his arm straight from his body, but when he opened his eyes he saw only Delia. She had wrenched the wicked KA-BAR from his shoulder. Confusion flooded his mind. Delia sat astride him with the bloody KA-BAR held tightly in both hands. She trembled, probably with fear. She swung the knife at his face, but Francis's right hand came up and smashed into her jaw, knocking her to the floor of the mower and sending the KA-BAR tumbling to the ground.

"It's okay, baby," he gasped weakly, "we're together now. You're back where you belong."

Delia's upper body hung off the side of the mower and she scrambled to escape. He tried to grab her by the legs but she wriggled the rest of the way off the mower.

"Delia, stop this. You're free now, free to be mine! We can finish this together." He flopped off the mower and crawled after her, dizzy and bleeding profusely.

***

Delia scrambled through the grass. Her chest was heaving with frightened exertion. She'd had the element of surprise but somehow she found herself losing this battle. She crawled on hands and knees over the hard earth away from the mower. Then her hand pressed onto something cold and sharp. She cried out in pain and picked up the fillet knife she'd dropped when she leapt onto the mower. Her heart raced and she closed bloody fingers over the knife.

With renewed determination, she prepared to stand and fight, but just then she heard Alice scream.

"Delia, look out!"

Francis pounced.

***

He landed on top of Delia, striking her hard across the face with his mushed-up hand. He yelled as he hit her, because it hurt and because he didn't want to hit his wife. *She should mind me without being punished.*

Her head lolled to the side for a moment then snapped back toward him, her eyes alight with a ferocious anger. *She's always been feisty.*

He tried to pin her down but she rolled out from under him. He fell to his side then pulled himself to his feet.

He took two shambling steps toward her and tried to grab her by the back of the hair, but Delia spun around. She had something shiny in her hand. The steel flashed in the sun as Delia swung, and the fillet knife cut across his cheek, biting into the skin and peeling it off over his jawbone. He howled in pain, half of his face flapping uselessly.

He tried to tell her, he tried to speak, but his voice came out muddy and distant.

"A promise, a promise is forever Delia." Blood poured from his shoulder and his face while he staggered forward.

Delia kept shaking her head. She still didn't understand.

His head rolled around on his shoulders, blood streaming off his jaw. He tried to focus on her. His eyes were blurry.

She held the knife with both hands, swaying back and forth like one of those tennis players waiting for the ball. His blood covered the filet knife. For just a moment, he saw a glint of his own reflection in the blade, then she jerked forward.

Her whole body pitched with the thrust. The fine steel plunged into his neck as if it were made of jelly.

He tried to make some sounds. They might have been words, but Delia wrenched the knife and his life gushed out of his neck and down over his twisted torso. The bloody waterfall soaked them both. Francis's last thoughts were of Delia.

She was supposed to be mine.

***

Delia dug the shovel into the dirt once more and Alice pulled her legs free, then fell against her. She held on tightly, then Alice stiffened against her.

"Alice, what is it?"

Alice didn't answer, but stared behind Delia with her jaw agape. Delia spun around, then dropped to her knees. Her own mouth dropped open in awe.

A shadowy figure stood before them, just barely there, a smoky, thin material but absolutely real. The women watched it approach with slow, fluid movements. Then it knelt down next to Delia and Alice.

Delia reached out to it. She knew the shadow had given her the strength and speed to save Alice.

"Thank you so much," she whispered.

In response, the shadow extended an arm to touch her hand. When they met, Delia felt a shock, then a tingle up through her arm. The shadow dissolved before her, and a new apparition took its place.

Kneeling in front of Delia and Alice, with her arm outstretched, was Delia's mother. She wore a small, sad smile.

"Mother," Delia gasped, her eyes wide and confused.

She nodded to Delia.

The whispers she'd only ever heard in her head rang out clearly now.

"Oh my God Dee, I hear it, too." Alice held tight to Delia and they both listened as her mother spoke.

"He will be back. Go far away from here. Do not return. He will hunt for you always."

"Francis? How can he come back? Like you did?"

Her mother nodded.

"Has it been you in my head all this time? Have you been trying to keep me safe?"

"It's all a mother wants to do." She still wore the sad smile. "I have to go now, dear."

"But I want to stay with you, Mother," Delia cried out. She felt like a child again, overwhelmed with a need to be held, to be comforted. She wanted to share so much with her mother, if she could only stay.

Her mother shook her head. "I will always be here for you," she said, and pointed toward Delia's chest. "Goodbye, child. I love you."

Delia and her mother had never been very close in her early life. Her mother cleaned the house and cooked the meals and set Delia to her chores, so there wasn't always much time for 'I love yous.' As her mother faded away into the wind, Delia whispered her goodbye.

"I love you, mother."

***

Delia wanted to take Alice straight to the hospital in Grand Rapids. Alice, however, was nearly back to her old self and had other plans. Once she had been freed from her earthen tomb, Alice staggered into Francis's house looking for water. Exhausted and dehydrated, Alice downed two glasses of lukewarm, rust-colored well water immediately.

Two minutes later, she'd found the liquor cabinet. After four fingers of whiskey in a dirty glass, she looked like the calm, composed but filthy Alice that Delia loved.

"We're going to the funeral, Dee."

"What? You need to go to the hospital."

"Absolutely not. I came here to meet Deb and Lilly and you came to say goodbye to your uncle. We're going and that's final."

Delia opened her mouth to argue but Alice cut her off.

"I got buried alive and nearly killed by your crazy ex. It's gonna be my way today!"

Delia had to smile. This was her Alice, all right. "Fine, but you look terrible. We had better go change, and I'm gonna bathe you."

"Perfect," Alice purred.

"What should we do with him?"

***

Jason LaVelle

Delia and Alice arrived at the funeral with all the style two women who had narrowly escaped murder could manage. They buried Francis in the grave he himself had dug for Alice. They didn't call the police, and had a feeling—a hope—that he wouldn't be missed.

Delia cried at Don's funeral, but not out of sadness for Don's passing. Her adoptive father had gone to the heavens, and he would always be missed, but Delia cried tears of joy that she could still stand next to her lover, hold her hand, and live for another day.

The priest said kind words, and the crowd lined up to drop flowers into Uncle Don's grave. Lilly was there, too, and gorgeous beyond compare. She stood next to her mother, her head bowed. As the crowd of mourners dispersed, Lilly rushed up to Delia and threw hers arms around her.

"My sister!" she cried into Delia's neck.

Even as an adult, Lilly had remained much smaller than Delia, and once again Delia remembered how good it felt to be a big sister. Lilly radiated goodness, and as she pulled away, her infectious smile caused Delia's eyes to light up.

"I've missed you so much."

"I've missed you too, little one."

A silence followed before Lilly motioned toward Alice with her eyes.

"Lilly, meet Alice. She's my—partner in life."

Lilly didn't miss a beat. She threw her arms around Alice. "I'm so happy to meet you!" she said, her words filled with sincerity.

"So, I guess we have some catching up to do, huh?" Lilly said, her eyes twinkling as she looked between Delia and Alice.

Delia sighed and pulled Lilly in for another long embrace. "I can't wait. But let's do it over a drink, honey. It's been a hell of a day."

Epilogue

It took almost two weeks for someone to report Francis missing to the police. Not out of concern for Francis, but for their order of three butchered pigs, which they now had no hope of reclaiming. The sheriff came out to the butcher's house, cringing as he exited the car. A foul odor had settled over the property, the odor of decay. It didn't take the sheriff long to cover the grounds.

The place had been messy for as long as he could remember, but nothing seemed out of the ordinary, save for one missing war veteran. The large mound of decaying carcasses in the back of the barn made Sheriff Rose very glad he stopped using the butcher after his father passed away. *Fucking disgrace, is what it is.* Tools and bits of mechanical parts lay scattered all about the porch, and the rusting riding tractor that had once been a prize in these parts had been left abandoned in the patchy, uneven yard.

Not much to investigate. The cooler still ran, and, judging by the state of the house, Francis hadn't been around for a while. *Might have wandered out into the woods and offed himself.* The sheriff had always gotten a bad feeling from the butcher's youngest son, even as a boy. He didn't make any further inquiries. Quite frankly, he didn't care. The sheriff pulled out a heavy box of steaks from the cooler, loaded them into his trunk, and drove home.

He never saw Francis's brother Larry hanging in the dimly lit cooler. Nor did he notice the section of lumpy ground covered with slightly fewer weeds than the rest of the lawn. A few weeks later, the electric company shut down the power and an awful stink went up around the farm. Months went by, and a lightning strike set the house ablaze, taking three acres of land with it, scorching the entire farm down to the earth.

Author's Note

While this is a work of fiction, and their names have been changed, Delia and Alice were actual people. They lived, loved, and fought for each other. They went to war for our country, and came home only to find that they must battle against a society that would never truly accept them. Love overcomes all. Love is our greatest hope, and sometimes our most powerful weapon in a hateful world. So please, love your neighbor, even if you don't understand them.

Acknowledgements

To all of my friends, thank you so much for your help and support in making this novel come together. It was a tough project to write, and without the advice and brutal honesty from all of you, it never would have come to life. To my fantastic team of beta readers: Heather, Amber, Betsy, Kate, Susan, Alexia and Terah; thank you so much, I really could not do this without you. My amazing editor Jessica took this manuscript and turned it into something great, I will be forever grateful for your advice and expertise. Most especially I'm grateful for my wife. Through long hours of writing, frustration, tears, and finally joy, she has supported me and made it possible for me to pursue my writing dreams. You are the best, Heather, I love you.

About the Author

Jason LaVelle is an author and photographer from West Michigan. When he's not spending time with his beautiful wife and four children, LaVelle works at a veterinary clinic, helping animals of all kinds. With his two pugs, Dragon and Mr. Sparkles, his Chihuahua, Mari, English Bulldog, Harley, and his annoying dachshund, Lady, he pretty much lives in a zoo.

After he's done playing with the dogs and tucking the kids into bed, he ventures down into the basement, where his umbrella cockatoo, Bella, whispers in his ear like a demonic muse, forcing him to explore the paranormal world inside his mind.

For more, please visit Jason LaVelle online at:
Website: www.darkhorsestudios3.wixsite.com/lavelle
Goodreads: Jason_N_Lavelle
Facebook: LaVelleBooks
Twitter: @TheJasonLaVelle
Instagram: TheJasonLaVelle

What's Next?

Watch for the next two books in the "A Dark Night Thriller" series to release as follows:

Book 2: *The Cold Room* – October 2018
Book 3: *The Dark of Night* – November 2018

More from Evolved Publishing

We offer great books across multiple genres, featuring hiqh-quality editing (which we believe is second-to-none) and fantastic covers.

As a hybrid small press, your support as loyal readers is so important to us, and we have strived, with tireless dedication and sheer determination, to deliver on the promise of our motto:
QUALITY IS PRIORITY #1!

Please check out all of our great books, which you can find at this link:
www.EvolvedPub.com/Catalog/

Thank you!

CPSIA information can be obtained
at www.ICGtesting.com
Printed in the USA
LVHW090459210219
608298LV00001B/90/P